"Let's make a deal. You must be used to those. You must understand, Zach—there must be something in this for me. Otherwise, I'm off."

He looked down at her, reluctant to grant any favors. But she knew that his love for his son would win the day.

"Done!" he said decisively. "But let's get this clear. It's just for a month."

"Agreed."

"No riotous parties."

"No."

Had he come a step closer? It seemed the gap between them had filled with a thick and electrifying heat.

"Next weekend, as part of your duties...I thought...maybe a boat trip."

She closed her eyes and nodded dumbly. And then she felt something brush her lips. Something warm. Soft yet firm. Every fiber of her being was crying out for Zach to touch her, hold her and make passionate love to her....

MISTRESS TO A MILLIONAIRE

*She's his in the bedroom,
but he can't buy her love...*

The ultimate fantasy becomes a reality.

Live the dream with more
MISTRESS TO A MILLIONAIRE titles
by some of your favorite
Harlequin Presents® authors.

Sara Wood

IN THE BILLIONAIRE'S BED

MISTRESS
TO A
MILLIONAIRE

HARLEQUIN®

TORONTO • NEW YORK • LONDON
AMSTERDAM • PARIS • SYDNEY • HAMBURG
STOCKHOLM • ATHENS • TOKYO • MILAN • MADRID
PRAGUE • WARSAW • BUDAPEST • AUCKLAND

ISBN 0-373-12377-9

IN THE BILLIONAIRE'S BED

First North American Publication 2004.

Visit us at www.eHarlequin.com

Printed in U.S.A.

CHAPTER ONE

'Hi, everyone.'

Catherine tried to sound bright but failed. As she eased her narrow boat alongside Tom's massive Dutch barge she could see from her friends' faces that the rumours she'd heard in Saxonbury town were probably true.

Tom, Steve, Nick and Dudley rose from the spacious well of the foredeck, looking alarmingly sympathetic. That made things worse. Her stomach did an impromptu roll of its own accord.

Now she had to face the fact that if Tresanton Island *had* been sold then her immediate future lay in the hands of the new owner.

Turning her head, she looked back longingly at the beautiful island further up river. She'd had no legal right to be there, even though she'd had the mooring for the past three years. That hadn't mattered with the tolerant and genial Edith Tresanton as her landlady. But ever since Edith's death there had been an air of uncertainty about her situation.

Willing hands caught the ropes she tossed. Hitching up her long skirt, she let The Boys—as she called them—haul her on board. Her gypsy-black pre-Raphaelite hair escaped from its binding and she deftly fastened it again, her sweet, fragile-boned face an unusual pallor.

'Been talking about you,' Tom said in greeting. 'Cuppa?'

She shook her head and perched apprehensively on the

deck lid. Steve gave her a friendly kiss and wasted no time getting to the point.

'You know the island's got a new owner?' he asked anxiously.

Her heart sank. 'I suspected it. That means I could be in trouble,' she said, her hopes disappearing into her tiny size three's. She rubbed suddenly damp palms on the thin cotton of her flowing skirt. 'What do you know?' she asked. 'Have the people moved in? I didn't see a car on the bank when I came past.'

'Removal van's been and gone. Local traders say a bossy, yuppie London woman's taken it over,' Tom answered, spiralling Catherine's spirits down still further. 'Fancy yuk-yellow sports car, all chrome and turbo thrust and so's she. City suit, egg-whisk hair, killer heels and an elaborately painted face.'

'Not exactly a kindred spirit,' she muttered.

She'd hoped that a nature lover would buy Tresanton Island. Who else would want somewhere so isolated, so rural? A nature lover would have liked having narrow boats around. Would have considered it romantic. The new owner didn't sound as if she'd be too empathetic.

'Yeah. Not our sort—or Edith's,' he grunted. 'A really bossy type. She's moved her stuff in and cleaned everyone out of expensive gourmet provisions—after screeching with shock-horror because Saxonbury doesn't stock wheat grass.' He grinned. 'Some bright spark directed her to a field for the grass and she went ballistic, calling him an ignorant peasant! That's all we know.'

Catherine managed a smile then released a huge breath of resignation. It sounded as though there would definitely be changes to the island—and to Edith's house. The manor's charming, countrified air would probably be transformed with the addition of a stainless steel kitchen and futuristic technology. And the island laid to lawn.

But what of her? Her wistful gaze lingered on her boat's scarlet cabin roof cluttered with flower boxes, assorted chimneys and narrow boat paraphernalia. Traditional in style and wonderfully cosy, the narrow boat had been the ideal solution for somewhere cheap to live and work in an expensive area. In all her twenty-six years she'd never felt so insecure.

'Yellow car's coming along the lane,' warned Steve, making everyone sit up sharply.

The colour screamed its yellowness so successfully that it was visible half a mile away. They watched it bumping slowly along. Catherine's heart bumped too. By the time she motored back to the island and moored her boat the new owner would be in residence.

She stood up shakily, her mouth set. Perhaps she'd be allowed to stay. Edith had let her have a small patch of ground for growing vegetables. And she'd liked to see Catherine's chickens roaming freely. Maybe this yuppie owner would be equally charmed.

'Thanks for the information,' she said, determined to fight her corner. 'I'd better introduce myself and see where I stand. There's no point in hanging around and imagining what's going to happen to me.'

'Want us to come as your "heavies"?' suggested Steve, flexing his muscles and adopting a mock-belligerent pose.

She smiled gratefully. Each one of them had helped her enormously in the early days, when the workings of a narrow boat were a mystery to her. All The Boys were poor, but they had good hearts and would do anything for her.

Dwarfed by Steve, she rested her small hand on the thin sleeve of his hole-ridden jumper and made a mental note to knit him another before winter came. If she was still there…

'I'll let you know,' she replied. 'First I'll appeal to her better nature. But keep the knuckle-dusters handy in case she hasn't got one,' she joked feebly.

'Get into her good books. Find her some wheat grass,' suggested Tom drily.

She gave a shaky little laugh. 'Fat chance!'

'And if she says your clients can't use the bridge, or tells you to go?' Steve asked.

She sucked in a wobbly breath. They all knew that moorings were like rocking horse droppings. Non-existent.

The thought hit her like a punch in the stomach. It would be the end of her idyllic life. Hello grotty flat in some crime-ridden ghetto. And she felt panic setting in because it would take years to build up her client-base again.

'I'd have no choice but to leave,' she answered.

'Good luck,' the men chorused with sympathy as she clambered back on board and cast off.

'Thanks,' she managed to choke out.

Remarkably, she focused her mind on the tricky task of doing the watery equivalent of a three-point-turn where the river widened. With her stomach apparently full of jitterbugging butterflies competing for the World Title, she straightened the boat up and headed for home on the far side of the island.

Luck? She let out a low groan. Judging from the information about the new owner she'd need something nearer to a miracle.

CHAPTER TWO

ZACHARIAH TALENT didn't notice the sheet of bluebells which were generously trying to obliterate the woodland floor. In fact, he didn't even register the existence of the wood itself.

Similarly, hedgerows passed by in a blur of white May blossom, while the verges quite fruitlessly boasted stately pink foxgloves, rising like rockets above the masses of buttery primulas.

City man from the top of his expensively cut dark hair to his polished black shoes, Zach remained oblivious to any of these rural delights.

'Pretty countryside. Shame about the yokels. They're dire, I can tell you. Look at that idiot,' his PA remarked sarcastically, swerving to avoid a lone walker.

'Uh,' Zach grunted.

Without looking up from the laptop computer balanced on his knees, he continued to read off a succession of figures into his mobile phone, his trade-mark frown drawing his hard dark brows together.

'Nearly there, Zach,' the soignée Jane cooed breathily. 'Isn't it exciting?'

Sharply he put Hong Kong on hold and glanced at his PA. She flashed him a smile that seemed worryingly warm. Never one to mix business with pleasure, he met it with his habitual, emotionless stare, his grey eyes cold and forbidding.

Was it happening again? he thought bleakly. And, if so, why did the women he worked with always imagine themselves in love with him? It wasn't as if he gave them any encouragement. Far from it. He couldn't be more distant if he tried.

'It's just a house. Bricks and mortar. An investment,' he said curtly.

'Oh, it's more than that!' she declared, alarming him even further with the mingled look of rapture and slyness on her face. 'It has real character. A home for a *family*.' There was a significant pause during which his irritation level increased several notches and then, in the absence of any comment from him, Jane hurried on. 'It needs modernising, of course. Better facilities all round. But the potential's there. Huge, airy rooms to set off your elegant antiques and furnishings—and its grounds run down to the River Saxe—'

'So you said,' he interrupted, cutting off her estate agent eulogy in mid-flow.

Mentally noting that he might soon have to advertise for a new PA, Zach dealt with his ringing phone, bought a tranche of well-priced bonds on the Hong Kong market and closed a profitable deal on some utilities shares.

'Have you any idea *why* Mrs Tresanton left you the house in her will?' Jane ventured curiously when he'd wrapped the call.

'No relatives. No one close,' he replied in his usual curt manner.

But it had been a surprise and he still had no idea why Edith had favoured him. He wasn't exactly the country type.

To avoid Jane's unsettling dreamy expression, he looked out of the window and scowled because his headache was getting worse.

The scenery seemed to leap at him, demanding his attention. He had an impression of an explosion of greenery that was almost unnerving.

They were driving along a pot-holed lane beside the river which looked utterly still and so smooth that it could have been enamelled the same blue as the sky. Saxe blue perhaps, he thought idly. He remembered that Edith had often talked of its beauty and had nagged him to call. There'd never been the time, of course.

She had been a good client of his. Almost a mother to him. His mouth tightened in an effort to control the bitter memory of his own mother's death seventeen years ago, a few months after his father had suffered a fatal stroke.

Odd, how overpowering his grief had been. He'd been eighteen then, but had barely known his parents. They'd both worked so hard for his betterment that he'd been a latch-key kid from the age of five and used to looking after himself. But when they'd died he'd suddenly become truly alone in the world.

Perhaps that was why he had become fond of Edith. Normally he didn't get close to his clients, preferring to devote himself to managing their financial affairs as creatively and as securely as possible.

But Edith had been different. Although she'd mothered him with constant reprimands about his hectic work schedules, she'd also made him laugh with her odd, eccentric ways during their monthly meetings in London. And laughter was in short supply in his busy life.

'I hope you like the house,' Jane said a little nervously, parking her banana yellow Aston Martin on a small tarmac area beside the river. And more petulantly, 'I just wish you'd checked it over first, before asking me to arrange for all your stuff to be moved in.'

'No time free. Not with those back-to-back meetings in the States. I'm sure you've settled me in very well,' he retorted crisply, leaping out and looking around for Tresanton Manor.

To his surprise, there was nothing to be seen but the placid river, some black duck things with white blobs on their foreheads, clumps of trees and bushes on a nearby island and stretches of unkempt fields. Apart from the rather piercing trill of birdsong the place seemed eerily quiet. The lack of traffic bothered him. It had implications.

'So where is it?' he demanded, feeling decidedly out of place in his sharply tailored business suit and fashionable purple shirt.

Jane teetered a little on her spindly heels, equally incongruous in her formal jacket and tight skirt. Tighter than usual, he suddenly realised. And…had she ever shown cleavage before? Help, he thought. Trouble ahead.

'Er…the house is over the bridge.' Meekly she indicated the narrow plank affair that led from the bank to the island.

Zach's mouth fell open. He put a hand to his throbbing temple.

'Over…?' With difficulty he mastered his shock. 'You're not telling me that the house is on…an…*island*?' he asked with cold incredulity.

Jane looked at him in panic. 'Zach! You must have read the deeds! Tresanton Manor and Tresanton Island—'

'No!' He glared. How could she have ever thought this place was suitable? 'That's what I employ *you* for. To summarise everything. To identify the crucial points. And I think I'd call an island a crucial point, wouldn't you? Where's the road across?' he rapped out.

'There isn't one,' Jane replied in a small voice. 'We have to walk from here—'

'We *what*…? I don't believe this!' he muttered. 'You expect me to park my Maserati here in the open—*when I* eventually get it back from the garage—to be vandalised by any idle yob who passes?'

'I don't think it's that kind of area...' Jane began nervously.

'Every area is that kind!' Zach muttered, thoroughly disenchanted with Edith's house already. He could imagine what it would be like, stuck here on a wet wintry day with his bored son, unable to walk straight from an integral garage into the warmth of a welcoming house. Hell. Now what? He'd promised Sam a house with a garden. 'I can't stay here. I'll have to hunt for something else,' he added.

'But you can't do that, remember?'

Zach groaned. He recalled Edith's peculiar requirement, which had seemed typically nutty but acceptable at the time:

> ...bequeath Zachariah Talent my house and all its contents, to live in for at least a year, otherwise the house is to be given to the first person he sees when he sets foot on the island.

Unbelievable. The milkman could end up owning two million's worth of real estate! If there *was* a milkman in this uninhabited outback, he thought sourly.

'OK. So I'll come just on weekends and camp out,' he growled.

He couldn't disappoint Sam. But this wasn't what he'd had in mind at all. He wanted proximity to burger bars, cinemas and zoos. How else did you entertain an eight-year-old?

'Jane!' he exclaimed suddenly. 'What the devil are those scruffy boats doing there?' he demanded, an extraordinary depth of disappointment making him want to lash out at anyone and anything.

She followed his scowl which directed her to the huddled boats, further down-river.

'Canal boats. Or are they called narrow boats? I believe Inland Waterways allows them to tie up there,' she replied helpfully.

Zach's mouth hardened like a trap. They'd be a security risk. Slowly he scanned the area, his expression becoming grimmer as he realised that Jane had also conveniently omitted to tell him that the house was in the middle of nowhere. The jagged pains in his head increased.

This was an unbelievable mess! He'd made a terrible mistake in delegating something this important!

Cursing himself for letting Jane handle everything, he was pragmatic enough to know that there wasn't much he could do for now.

All right. He'd grit his teeth and use the house on weekends for the required year, but no way was he going to rest until there were decent paths and safety rails to stop his son from falling into the river.

Nor was he going to live permanently on an island where goodness knew who could easily leap from a boat and merrily rob him of his entire art collection.

'Get on to the garage and have my car delivered here as soon as possible,' he rapped out. '*I'm* dealing with this mess personally, so cancel any engagements till further notice. I'll e-mail you with the improvements that I decide will be necessary before the house goes on the market. And find me something more suitable in the meantime where I can live and secure my valuables. In a city. Near restaurants. A gym. Theatres. Understand? Keys!' Peremptorily he held out his hand, knowing he was being unreasonably curt. 'Please,' he growled as the flustered Jane fumbled anxiously in her bag.

She was a good PA. But ever since she'd viewed Tresanton Manor there had been a light in her eye that had boded ill. She was ready to nest and he was in her sights. But he sure as hell wasn't going to choose sofas and curtains with anyone ever again.

Choking back an urge to rant and rail that his plans had gone awry and his son was unlikely to bond with him in this rural hell, he grabbed his laptop, bade Jane a curt goodbye and strode over the bridge, wondering with some desperation if he would ever win his son's love.

He'd been banking on this house to help achieve that goal. And only now did he realise how important it was to him that he was loved by his child. Of course, he'd talked about his son's indifference to Edith, but he'd never let her know how deeply he was hurt. Or even admitted it to himself.

He felt a heavy ache in his heart. Pain tightened his mouth and burned in his charcoal eyes. One day his son would hug him, he vowed, instead of treating him with cool reserve.

Women he could do without in his life. All the ones he'd met socially had rung up pound signs in their eyes when they knew who he was.

And none of the women he'd dated had been able to cope with the realities of his hectic work-load. Nor had his ex-wife. But he wanted to give his son financial security, and you didn't get rich—or stay rich—dancing attendance on females and taking them out shopping.

In a thoroughly bad mood at the collapse of his dreams, he stomped along the muddy path, occasionally ducking his head to avoid being attacked by the boughs of apple trees. You didn't have such problems with pavements.

He couldn't understand why Edith had thought she was doing him a favour by forcing him to live here for a year. How could she call this place a paradise? he wondered grumpily.

And then he noticed the woman.

CHAPTER THREE

SHE was walking ahead of him through the orchard. No, drifting. He stopped dead in his tracks, brought up short by what he saw.

She must have heard his approach because, slender as a flexing wand, she slowly turned to face him, her small face so delicate and fey that he wondered if he was hallucinating. Tiny and graceful, she stood up to her ankles in a sea of buttercups and she looked as though she had just stepped out of a medieval illustration.

Not normally fanciful, he tried to understand why he'd had this impression. It could have been her long, close-fitting skirt flaring out from below the knee, or the long-sleeved soft cream top that hugged her slim figure like a second skin.

Or perhaps it was the hair that made her look like a modern day Guinevere. It was black and cascaded in thick waves down her lissom back from an imprisoning twist of…

He narrowed his eyes in surprise. She'd caught up her hair at the nape of her long neck with a rope of living greenery. Ivy, or something. Entwined with real flowers. Weird.

A hippie flower child, he decided, and scowled. Maybe from one of those boats. Spying out the land. Instinctively he fingered the scar on his forehead.

After the unpleasant experience of a burglary and two muggings—one of which had involved a woman who'd diverted his attention with a plausible sob story—he'd

17

learnt to be suspicious where itinerant strangers were concerned. Even medieval hippies as tiny as this one.

In London you didn't look strangers in the eye. Never wore an expensive watch. Walked quickly everywhere, locked your car while driving, kept the car revved at traffic lights and stayed alert at all times. That's how you survived in the City.

'You're on my land!' he growled, deliberately projecting menace.

Her placid expression didn't alter. She remained very still and calm, as if waiting for him to approach. Much to his surprise, he did. Usually people came to him.

As he glowered his way towards her a small hand came out in a meek greeting.

'I'm Catherine Leigh. How do you do?'

It was a sweet, gentle voice and before he knew it he had taken the dainty, fluttering fingers in his and was muttering less irritably, 'Zach Talent.'

Had he noticed how nervous she was? Hastily she retracted her fingers from the firm, decisive grip and clasped them behind her back so that he didn't see how badly they were shaking.

'You...said this was *your* island,' she began huskily, her face puzzled.

'Apparently it is,' he replied, his mouth clamping shut into a hard, exasperated line as if that fact didn't please him one bit. His intimidating frown deepened and it seemed that his eyes glinted with shards of icy anger.

'Oh!'

She considered this, deciding that she'd rather deal with the woman with egg-whisk hair and killer heels than this elegantly clad grouch. Then she brightened. The woman must be his wife. Better to wait and talk to her.

'Are you on your own?' asked the owner of the frown.

He turned to scan the undergrowth as if marauding bandits might leap out at any minute.

'Yes. Just me,' she replied quietly.

'Hmm.' He relaxed his guard a fraction. 'So what are you doing here?' he shot out.

'I came to speak to your wife,' Catherine told him with absolute truth.

'Did you?' He sounded unconvinced for some inexplicable reason.

She continued to gaze at him with a pleasant, noncommittal expression on her face and was relieved to see the deep line between his brows easing a little. She noticed a long scar on his forehead and wondered apprehensively how he'd acquired it.

'Can I see her? Is she in?'

'No.'

How to win friends and influence people, she thought drily. He really was the most surly of men!

'Then I think I'll come back later when she's at home,' she suggested gravely.

'No, you don't. *Wait!*' The command was barked out just as she turned to go.

Caught off-guard as she whirled around, her wide-eyed look of utter surprise seemed to take him unawares too. For a split second she thought his steely eyes had softened to a misty grey.

Then she realised it must have been a trick of the light. When she looked again they were hard and shuttered with no hint of his feelings at all.

'You'll talk to *me*,' he said sharply. 'Let's see if you can come up with a convincing excuse for being here.'

'Of course I can!' she replied in surprise, not allowing herself to be riled by his rudeness.

'In that case, I'm not standing here knee-deep in muck,' he exaggerated. 'Come to the house.'

Without waiting for her response to this arrogant order, Zach Talent strode off down the path, his shiny leather shoes squelching in the mud.

Catherine hesitated and then, before she knew it, she was following. She felt almost as if she had been drawn by a magnet. And as she walked and marvelled at the man's compelling authority she ruefully prepared to tug her forelock. A lot.

She heaved a sigh. Somehow she felt it wouldn't help even if she tugged out handfuls of hair in the process.

Zach was clearly one of those suspicious types who imagined everyone was trying to pull a fast one. He'd looked at her as if she might be planning something evil.

From his manner, she reckoned that he also liked to be in control. He wasn't the kind of man to do anyone a favour. For him, she suspected that it would be a matter of honour not to show any sign of weakness by granting concessions to any passing peasant.

Anxiously she studied his taut body as he strode rapidly along, rocketing out staccato orders to someone on his mobile phone as if every second and every word was precious and not to be wasted by adding pleasantries.

With gloom in her heart, she hurried after him through Edith's—Zach's!—beautiful wild-life garden. And she wondered how long it would be before Killer Heels and The Frown strimmed every blade of grass within an inch of its life and installed soulless carpet bedding. Perhaps even artificial turf and security lights. With a helipad.

She mourned for the island's bleak future. Lifting her bowed head, she listened to the insistent warble of a blackcap, high on its perch in a lemon-scented azalea. It was joined by the unmistakable trill of a robin, singing its heart out from an oak tree.

Ring doves were cooing lovingly from the gnarled old mulberry tree and occasionally she heard a watery scuffle as a mallard drake enthusiastically courted a lady friend.

She and Zach were making their way through the rhododendron walk. Here, the peeling trunks arched over their heads like arms reaching out to embrace one another. In a few weeks the walk would be a blaze of colour.

The perfume of the lilies of the valley beneath made her catch her breath in wonder and she believed that, although Zach's ear was still attached to his phone, even he had slowed his relentlessly brisk stride to savour the beauty of the garden.

Still holding her breath, she waited till he reached the glade. And was pleased to see that he had stopped, briefly looking around. But her pleasure was short-lived. When she quietly came to stand beside him, she realised that the man was a heathen after all.

'Sell,' he was curtly instructing some hapless minion, his hand massaging the back of his neck abstractedly. 'And let's have your investment strategy for the Far East by the end of the day...'

Barbarian! Infuriated by his insensitivity, she firmly shut him out. They were on different planets. This could be the last time she enjoyed the poignantly familiar sight that met her eyes, and she wanted to savour it to the full.

Bluebells had colonised the grassy glade, creating a sea of sapphire waves as the breeze stirred the nodding bells. The blossom-laden branches of ancient apple and pear trees bowed down almost to the shifting patches of blue, but where the path ran, ornamental Japanese cherry trees formed a vista to the house.

Framed dramatically, and with the shedding cherry

blossom fluttering to the ground like confetti before it, the lovely Georgian manor house basked in the sun, its honey stone walls glowing as if they'd been dipped in liquid gold.

Entranced, she looked up at Zach for his reaction, hoping that he'd been stirred by the glory of it all. But with his frown resolutely in place he was intently tapping in a new number on his wretched mobile.

'Tim? About those Hedge Funds,' he growled, giving his mud-spattered shoes a basilisk stare.

She despaired, doubting that the funds were a charitable donation to the preservation of England's beautiful country hedges.

He'd seen nothing. Not the rich dark throats of the dazzling white azaleas brushing his jacket, or the ladies fingers, violets, forget-me-nots and scarlet pimpernel which were shyly peeping from the undergrowth beside the path.

Deaf to everything but the grinding machine of business, he'd heard nothing of the jubilant birds filling the island with sweet song. And he was too busy sniffing out a deal to register the mingled fragrances that drifted on the slight breeze, or the musty, warm aroma that arose from the leaf litter in the surrounding woodland.

Edith's heaven was totally lost on him. Catherine watched sadly as he strode on, discussing High Fidelity Bonds instead of being alive to the wonders of the natural world around him. She felt a wave of sadness jerk at her chest. He would never love this place as she did.

It was small consolation that he hadn't ploughed straight through the bluebells, but had skirted the edge. He wasn't a total heathen then. But she could see that he would have no empathy for Edith's carefully rampant style of gardening.

Zach and his wife were obviously people with different

values and priorities. Sophisticates, who lived the fast life of the City.

Catherine knew instinctively that they would definitely *not* approve of the way she earned her living. Nor would they be sympathetic towards a woman who chose to live on a boat like a water gypsy.

Her face fell. She might as well accept now that she'd probably be hurled out on her ear. She'd be obliged to wander the rivers and canals of England until she found a vacant mooring that she could afford. And then she'd have to start building up her clientele all over again.

She bit her lip, trying to stop herself from crying with frustrated anger. And she wondered crossly why this man had taken on Tresanton Manor when it was so patently wrong for him.

With her ears assailed by a barrage of fast-paced business deals which broke the gentle, monastic peace of the magical garden, she trudged silently towards the house she loved, aching to think that not only would she be leaving the island and all her friends, but that a Philistine and his wife would be ignorant of its joys.

She had to try to persuade him that there were benefits in having someone around to keep an eye on things. But in her heart she knew that she didn't stand a chance.

Oh, Edith! she sighed. If you only knew who was about to desecrate your lovely island!

CHAPTER FOUR

'ALL these keys!' Grumbling, Zach was turning the huge bunch in his hand, trying to find the one that opened the main door.

'It's like this one,' Catherine said with commendable patience.

Tiredly she lifted the rope line at her waist and selected Edith's key from the others for comparison.

Zach stiffened. 'You have a *key*?' he barked in staccato consternation, as if she'd committed a crime. Or was about to.

'I often came to see the previous owner,' she explained, her spirits at an all-time low. 'She gave me one to let myself in.'

Zach's eyes narrowed and fixed on her like heat-seeking missiles.

'Have you been in the house since she died?' he shot out suspiciously.

Bristling, she regarded him with the level and reproving gaze of a Victorian schoolmistress confiscating jelly beans from a naughty child.

'You mean have I nipped in to steal anything?' she flung back haughtily. 'Brass fittings? A marble fireplace or two? A staircase, maybe?'

'It happens.' He didn't seem embarrassed by her bluntness. 'Though I suppose you're not likely to admit to theft.'

His audacity was breathtaking. Catherine inhaled

deeply. It was that or hit him and she didn't believe in violence.

'I haven't stolen anything. In fact, I haven't set foot in the house since I found Edith in her bed,' she informed him, the faint tremor in her voice betraying how painful that discovery had been.

'*You* found her?' He seemed to be on the verge of saying something—his sympathies, perhaps—but, thought Catherine darkly, he managed to stop himself in time from doing anything so remotely human. Instead, he grunted. 'Hmm. I'll have to take your word for it, then,' he muttered, but his eyes lingered on her tremulous mouth thoughtfully.

'Or you could ask around,' she said, tightening her lips in a rare display of anger, 'and then you'd learn that I don't have a dishonest bone in my body!'

To her discomfort, he examined her with clinical detail, as if to check how honest her bones might be. His intense scrutiny brought a flush to her face and she lowered her startled nut-brown eyes to avoid his road-driller stare.

'Don't think I won't do that,' he snapped.

Her mutinous gaze flashed up to his again. 'Can't you read faces? Don't you realise the kind of person I am?'

He seemed to flinch and withdraw into himself. The hard and impenetrable coldness he was projecting made her shiver, as if she'd stepped into cold storage.

'I make it a habit never to trust anyone until I have overwhelming proof of their integrity.'

'You must find it hard to make friends,' she observed drily.

His gaze burned angrily into her. 'I'd like that key,' he growled.

With her own dark eyes conveying her scorn, she eased

it off the cork float that had twice saved her boat keys from sinking to the bottom of the river.

OK. She'd blown it. But she wouldn't be bullied. If standing up to this monster meant that she'd have to leave, then that would have to be her fate.

She had never disliked anyone before, always finding good in everyone she met. But this guy was without any decent characteristics at all.

And he owned Edith's island! Conquering her misery, she tipped up her small chin in a direct challenge.

'Take it.' She thrust the key at him. 'I won't be needing it any more,' she bit out, stiff with indignation.

'Darn right you won't,' he muttered, taking it from her.

Tossing back her tumbling hair and with protesting cherry blossom falling from the ivy tie, she took an angry intake of breath. She felt close to breathing out fire and brimstone and melting Zach Talent where he stood!

'No. You're no Edith, breathing sweetness and light. So I doubt that I'll be popping in to play gin rummy with you,' she snapped, 'or to help you patch your sheets or paint rainbows in the bathroom!'

Clearly astonished by her outburst, he hooked up an eyebrow and stared deeply into her defiant eyes—which rounded in confusion when she felt something go *bump* somewhere in the region of her heart. Shocked, she pressed a fluttering hand to her breast in bewilderment.

An expression of liquid warmth eased the tautness of his face and then was gone. But in that brief flash, when vibrant life lit smoky fires in his grey eyes and the corners of his firm mouth lifted with hungry desire, she felt as though she'd been felled by a thunderbolt.

After a breathless second, while something hot and visceral seemed to link them both in its fatal flames, he spun furiously on his heel to plunge the key into the keyhole with brute force.

Quivering, she stood gazing in horror at his broad and powerful back while he struggled irritably with the tricky lock. What had all that been about?

Sex, she thought—the answer nipping with alarming boldness into her head. She cringed with mortification. Quite unexpectedly, she had discovered that fierce passions lurked beneath Zach Talent's granite exterior.

And, more shocking, within her, too. He was married! How *could* she?

The surging fizz of her blood, and the sense of danger and excitement which had electrified the air between them, was something she'd never known before. She had never believed such a force could exist—or that it might one day seek her out.

Love, she'd fondly imagined, would be a gentle, warm sensation. Like sinking into a deep bath. With love, would come the joy of eventually uniting with the person you trusted and adored above all other people. The union would be sweet and beautiful, a meeting of mind and body and soul. Two people expressing the totality of their love.

But she had been taken unawares by the effect of Zach's raw, sexual attraction. Never had she expected to feel this harsh, primeval urge of nature that owed nothing to love and everything to pure, animal instinct. It was humiliating that she should. And, given the fact that she knew his marital state, it demeaned her.

It only showed her innocence, she thought wryly, that she could be so easily zapped into a quivering mess by a rogue City trader—who was also her unwitting landlord!

How silly to be affected. He certainly hadn't known what he'd been doing, or that one unguarded and casual look from him could turn her insides out!

Men were supposed to think about sex every six seconds, she'd read. She supposed that she'd been in his eyeline at the time.

She made a face. How she pitied his wife! He'd be a terrible lover. He'd probably fit in his embraces between calls to New York and the London Stock Exchange!

Would he take his mobile to bed? she wondered, warming to her theme. Very likely, she conceded and her face relaxed into a broad grin at the thought of his wife's fury at being interrupted by a discussion on High Fidelity bonds at a crucial moment.

Stifling a giggle, she was relieved to find that her pulses had stopped careering about in hysteria and that her body had calmed down after its peculiar insurrection.

It had been a blip in her hormonal activity. The result of Zach's overwhelming good looks and perfect physique. Plus the frisson of being in close proximity with an Alpha male.

She was susceptible to superficial looks, it seemed. Well. If a man could ogle with impunity, so could she.

'You're smiling,' he accused gruffly.

He had pushed the door open and was standing back, waiting for her to enter. With understandable caution she flicked her amused eyes up to his and was horrified to find herself immediately swimming for her life.

'Isn't it allowed?' she retorted.

But her defiance was spoiled by a dismaying huskiness.

He shrugged. 'Be my guest. But share the joke. Or is it on me?' he asked suspiciously. And he searched around for bandits again.

She waved a deprecating hand.

'Forget it. You wouldn't understand!'

'Try me,' he said with underlying menace.

She read too much into that and found herself stupidly blushing.

'Absolutely not!'

What did he mean by saying the joke might be on him? Why was he so wary of her motives? Desperate to hide her flushed face, she hastily bent to remove her shoes before heading for the farmhouse kitchen, glad to sit down and give her jellied legs some relief.

'You do know your way around,' he drawled speculatively, appearing in his stockinged feet.

Nice feet, she noticed. High arches. Crossing one leg over the other, he leant, dark and brooding, in the doorway. And a curl of excitement quickened her breath.

So she gritted her teeth and said nothing. All her energies were concentrated on controlling her wilful hormones in case their eyes met while his brain was connecting with his loins again.

'Glad you made yourself at home,' he added with dry sarcasm.

Catherine jumped up. 'Oh! You must think I'm so rude. I'm sorry,' she said hastily, remembering her manners. This was his home now. She fixed him with her dark chocolate eyes, suitably apologetic. 'Forgive me,' she murmured contritely. 'It was force of habit.'

His intently focused stare was disconcerting. Something had happened to his mouth. It seemed to be fuller. Beautifully shaped. The tip of her tongue tasted her own lips as if in anticipation.

Wicked, wanton ideas flashed through her mind before she could stop them. Like putting her hands on his warm chest, standing on tiptoe and kissing those classically curved lips till he melted. Appalled beyond belief, she clamped down on the impulse ruthlessly.

Somehow she dragged her gaze away and lowered her

thick lashes, sick to the stomach by her runaway feelings. She felt bewildered by what was happening to her strong sense of morality.

'Habit? Does that mean you lived here at one time?' he asked in a slow kind of slur, quite different to his earlier speech. And so sexy as to set her nerves jangling. 'Or did you merely come to stay in the house?'

'No.' Hot and bothered, she struggled to regain the clarity of her voice. 'I've never lived here. Though Edith asked me to, a few months after we first met.'

Zach looked puzzled. 'And you refused?'

'I like my independence,' Catherine replied. 'I've lived alone for ten years, ever since I was sixteen. Edith understood, once I'd explained. Our friendship wasn't affected.'

'Did you know she had an extensive portfolio?' he shot out.

'Not unless you translate that for me,' she countered, annoyed by his City-speak. 'I only learnt English and French at school,' she added with rare sarcasm.

'She was very wealthy,' he drawled.

'Really? Are you sure?' she said in surprise. 'She lived very simply.'

'But she also owned this house and island,' he pointed out.

'Plenty of people live in big houses they've inherited— yet they're as poor as church mice. Places like this cost a great deal to keep maintained. If you see someone like Edith making economies, turning worn sheets sides to middle and rarely buying any clothes, you assume they're hard up,' Catherine retorted.

His sardonic eyes narrowed. 'Did she ever help you out financially?'

'Certainly not!' Catherine looked at him askance. 'She

wouldn't ever have been so crass! I stand on my own feet. I'd never respect myself otherwise!'

'But you were a frequent visitor and made yourself at home,' he probed.

'Yes. As a friend. When I called, I'd let myself in. Edith would be sitting there,' she explained, indicating the comfortable pine armchair on the opposite side of the big table. 'And I'd sit here.'

Her eyes were misty with memories when they looked up into his and met a blaze of answering fire.

There was a hushed pause while the air seemed to thicken and enfold them both. Catherine floundered. Some kind of powerful force was trying to draw her to him. She could hear the thudding of her heart booming in her ears.

Panicking, she lifted a fluttering hand to fiddle with her hair. The caress of his eyes, as she curled a strand around her ear, made her stomach turn to water.

At last he spoke, quietly and yet with a grating tone, as if something was blocking his throat.

'If you knew her well, then you might be able to help me.'

'Help you?' she repeated stupidly, playing for time while her brain unscrambled itself and began to rule her body again.

Almost vaguely, he glared at his trilling phone, immobilised it and clipped it on to his belt. Then he took a deep breath.

'Yes. But first I need a coffee,' he announced, brisk and curt once more. 'So, for a start, any idea where the kettle might be?'

'On the Aga.' Relieved to be involved in something practical, she pointed to the scarlet enamelled stove, one of Edith's few extravagances. 'I didn't turn it off. I thought it would be best if it was cosy and welcoming in here, for whoever came to view the house.'

He looked at the kettle uncertainly, as if he didn't know what to do with a piece of equipment that didn't hitch up to an electric socket. She took pity on him, deftly filling the kettle with water and carrying it to the hob.

Her skin prickled. He had come very close and was watching what she did. Slightly flustered by the invading infusion of heat in her body, she lifted the hob lid, put the kettle on the boiling plate then hurried over to the dresser.

As she lifted down the mugs her hand faltered and she stared blindly into space, thinking of the countless times she and Edith had chatted together at this very table.

'I've had groceries delivered,' Zach announced crisply, rummaging in the cupboards. 'It's a matter of finding them. Coffee do you as well?' He waved an expensive pack of ground coffee at her, only then noticing her mournful face. 'What's the matter?'

Catherine bit her lip and unearthed Edith's cafetière, selecting an herb tea for herself.

'I miss her,' she said softly, her eyes misting over again. It was odd. She rarely cried. But her emotions had been tested to the limit over the past ten days. And especially during the past hour. 'I miss her more than I could ever have imagined,' she blurted out.

'Hmm. You were very close, then?'

The low vibration of his voice seemed to rumble through her body. She shuddered, thinking that if this man ever turned his attention to a woman and opened up his emotions, she wouldn't have a chance.

'We were like mother and daughter. I was devastated to—to find her,' she whispered, making a hash of spooning the aromatic coffee into the pot.

The spoon was taken from her hand. For a moment their fingers were linked: warm, strangely comforting. Horrible flashes of fire attacked her loins and she snatched her hand away in appalled fury, turning her back on him and feeling stupidly like bursting into tears of utter shame.

'Mother and daughter,' Zach repeated in a voice rolling with gravel. She heard him suck in a huge breath. 'I'm sorry,' he said flatly. 'It's obvious that her death has touched you deeply.'

She hunched her slight shoulders and could only nod. She didn't want to break down in front of this hard-hearted stranger. But losing her beloved Edith, with all her merry, wacky ways, *plus* the prospect of never seeing the island again, just made her want to wail.

'I—I came to check on her every day. We'd have breakfast together,' Catherine mumbled painfully. She was torturing herself and she didn't know why she was confiding in someone she disliked so much, only that she had to do so. 'She made wonderful bread. We'd lather it with butter and home-made jam or marmalade and watch the birds demolishing our fat balls.'

Zach looked puzzled. 'Your what?'

'Fat. Impregnated with nuts and seeds,' she said listlessly. 'We melt the fat, stir in the nuts and so on and pour the mixture into pots till it sets. We—I—' she stumbled, '—only provide seed now.'

'Really?'

Feeling forlorn, Catherine gazed at the trees outside the window, adorned with bird feeders. Two long-tailed tits were currently availing themselves of the facility.

'Yes. You need to vary the food, depending on the time of year and whether the birds are nesting,' she advised absently.

'And you've been coming over here and doing this ever since Edith died,' he remarked with disapproval.

Dumbly, she nodded. 'Someone had to,' she mumbled, sensing that the birds would have to fend for themselves through the winter in future.

'You won't, of course, be doing that again,' said Zach sternly, confirming her worst fears. 'I value my privacy and I don't want people wandering about my land, particularly when I'm not here.'

She looked up, her eyes wide and watchful.

'Won't you be living here all the time, then?'

He grimaced as if he'd rather find a convenient cave in the Himalayas.

'No.'

'You don't like it, do you?'

'Not much.'

Presumably the wife had bought the house without his knowledge. What an odd thing to do. Unless his wife was the one with the money.

'Poor Edith,' she said quietly. 'She often said she had great plans for this place when she'd gone. But she'd never tell me what she meant. I didn't even know it was on the market.'

'It wasn't. She left it to me in her will.'

Catherine's mouth fell open in amazement. *'You?'* she gasped. 'I don't believe it! You weren't even at her funeral—'

'I don't go to them,' he said, with an odd tightening of his mouth.

There had been an ostentatious wreath, Catherine remembered, a sharp contrast to the country flowers she and her boating friends had placed on the coffin. The florist's card bore just one word. 'Farewell.' Not the most heartfelt message she'd ever seen, but typical of someone like Zach. And now she was intrigued.

'You were the lilies,' she said.

'I was the lilies,' he confirmed.

Catherine's eyes widened. Knowing Edith as she did, it seemed inconceivable that Zach and the old lady could have any point of contact!

'How would Edith ever know someone like you?' she wondered aloud.

'I run an investment company. I was her financial adviser and I managed her money.'

She nodded. *That* made sense. But Edith wouldn't have liked him enough to entrust her precious island to his smooth, City hands!

'Why would she give the island to you?' she asked in confusion. 'You're the last person on earth—'

She clamped her lips together. She'd said too much.

'You're right,' he said, his mouth curling in wry amusement. 'I don't understand either. For some wacky reason known only to Edith, she wanted me to live here.'

'But you must already have a house!' she declared, visualising an opulent mansion with four swimming pools and obsequious servants tugging their forelocks like crazy.

'No. A flat in London.'

And that, she thought, would suit him perfectly. Something in stainless steel with furniture that looked stylish but was hell to use, something in a smart and expensive district.

'Well, you can't *want* this island!' she argued.

'You're right. I don't.'

For a moment, Catherine felt a glimmer of hope. He'd off-load it on to someone else—someone more empathetic—and she'd have a better chance of persuading the next owner to let her stay.

'I see,' she said, perking up considerably. 'You'll put it on the market, then.'

'I don't discuss my business,' he replied cuttingly.

Suitably rebuked, Catherine nodded, still delighted that their acquaintance would probably be short and sour.

'I don't blame you,' she confided. 'The path gets horribly muddy in the winter. You can see what it's like now, even with the few showers we've had recently. And of course you're very isolated here.' She remembered the wheat grass. 'No city amenities. A distinct lack of exotic food.'

He gave her a thoughtful and searing look which suggested he knew exactly what she was up to.

'But despite all these problems, you…love it all,' he observed in a low tone.

Her eyes rounded. 'How do you know that?'

There was a pause, during which she noticed the increased rise and fall of his chest.

'The way you looked at the bluebells.' Apparently about to say something else, he cleared his throat instead.

'You noticed them, then?' she said drily.

'In passing.' Zach tilted his head to one side and gave her another speculative look. 'If you were as close to Edith as you claim,' he mused, 'why didn't she leave *you* the house and land?'

Catherine smiled, thinking of her conversation with the old lady.

'Oh, she said she was planning to do that. But I told her I didn't want it,' she answered solemnly.

He gave a snort of disbelief. 'I find that hard to accept,' he said scathingly.

'It was a practical decision. How would I afford to run it?' she argued.

'With her money, of course.'

'But I didn't know she had any!' Catherine protested.

'Odd that she didn't tell you,' he mused.

'I didn't give her a chance. I told her that I'd rattle around in Tresanton Manor on my own and feel lonely. And my friends might not come and visit me any more.'

'Why not?'

'Because they're ordinary people and they'd feel intimidated,' she said simply.

'You could have sold it.'

She stared, uncomprehending. 'What would be the point in being given a house and then immediately off-loading it?'

'Are you deliberately being provocative, or are you financially naïve?' he marvelled sarcastically. 'The point is that you would have made a lot of money.'

Money. It obviously ruled his life. Acquisitions, material possessions, they were all he saw, all he knew. Odd that she was so attracted to him. Perhaps it was the magnetism of opposites. Even now, alienated by his cold obsession with wealth, she felt an undeniable feral thrill from his extreme masculinity.

But where to start, to explain her philosophy of life? He wouldn't understand it for a moment. His eyebrow hooked up cynically as though she must be lying because she hadn't come up with an explanation. That galvanised her to give him one.

'Edith knew my views on living simply,' she said with quiet passion. 'I wouldn't want more money than I knew what to do with. Besides, I'd worry like mad if I had money invested in the stock market.'

'Think of all the new clothes you could have had,' he suggested.

'I have all I need! If I want something like a winter coat, I work extra hours. I already have a home that means a great deal to me. I truly have everything I want. Why should I rock the boat by changing my circumstances? I could end up very unhappy and out of my depth. Edith knew me well enough to know that quality of life is more important to me than material possessions. She accepted that because it was her philosophy too.' Catherine smiled fondly.

Clearly baffled, he shook his head. 'I don't understand.'

'No,' she said with a gentle sorrow. 'I don't suppose you do. But… Supposing I had accepted her offer. It would have changed the way people regard me, especially if she'd left me all her money too. As I said, my friends would have been ill at ease in the manor and very conscious of the differences in our situations. If I bought them a round of drinks in the pub, they might think I was being patronising. If I didn't, they'd think I was mean. You can't win. When someone's financial circumstances change, the attitude of people around them changes too. I have good friends, people I am very fond of,' she said, gazing up at him earnestly. 'I don't want to lose their unquestioning friendship. It means everything to me.'

'Living in an expensive house you'd soon make new friends,' he remarked cynically.

'Exactly! They would be drawn by my apparent wealth,' she cried with heartfelt passion. 'That's the last thing I want! My friendships are *genuine*. People like me for who I am, not *what* I am or how much money I've got. We do one another favours, which makes for a wonderful sense of community and protection. I am very happy and I'd be a fool to jeopardise that happiness. I explained all this to Edith and she realised that I already had…my…paradise.'

Her voice had faltered towards the end of the sentence. Any moment now and it could be Paradise Lost.

The kettle began to sing. Just in time, she managed to stop him from lifting it and burning his hand. Unfortunately her dash to the stove meant that they ended up body to body, his arms wrapping around her protectively when she cannoned into him.

'Hot,' she babbled breathily, her flapping hand indicating the kettle. But all she could feel was the fiery furnace of his chest. The frantic beating of her imprisoned heart. She was too shocked to move.

'Hot. I see,' he murmured, his mouth a sinful curve as his head seemed to bend low to hers.

Scorn laced her eyes. Another married man on the make, ready for any opportunity. Buster, she thought, your six seconds are up.

'I'll make the drinks,' she snapped, glaring at him.

The grey eyes chilled. The sinful curve disappeared and she was abruptly released.

'You do that.'

With elaborate care she filled the cafetière and placed it on the table. Then she added hot water to the herbal tea bag and slid, subdued, into her chair again.

Her pulses were galloping like a herd of wild horses. The man was so packed with rampant male hormones that he was a danger to her self-respect. She had to get away.

Her heart sank. That meant she must broach the subject of her mooring without any further beating about the bush.

She'd hoped to prepare the ground by chatting in a companionable way so that he felt at ease with her, and therefore more inclined to let her stay. But, she thought gloomily, a leisurely approach was out of the question now.

'Have you thought of a reason for wandering about my island?' he asked sardonically before she could come up with her opening line.

Her shoulders slumped. Not the most promising of starts.

'Edith let me moor my boat on the far side,' she began, deciding on a full frontal attack.

'What kind of a boat?' The frown was working hard as he pulled a pack of painkillers from inside his jacket and popped out two pills. 'Do you row over here from the village or something?'

Catherine wondered if his bad temper was due to his headache. He'd been rubbing his head a lot, she recalled.

'It's a narrow boat,' she explained. 'I live on it.'

His face was a picture. Hastily she took advantage of his astonishment.

'I was wondering, if temporarily—'

'No.'

She blinked. 'You haven't heard what I was about to say!'

'I'm not stupid. I make my living by putting two and two together. You want to continue the arrangement. The answer's no.'

'Surely, if you're going to sell—?'

'All the more reason to get rid of any illicit vagrants who call in whenever the fancy takes them.'

Her face flamed at the description. 'But it's—!'

'No.'

Her mutinous gene seemed to assert itself. 'Why?' she demanded, her eyes blazing with anger.

Zach's gaze dropped, his thick black lashes a heart-stopping crescent on his cheeks as he pushed down the cafetière plunger slowly then poured out the coffee, filling the kitchen with its rich aroma.

'Nobody would buy this place with itinerants tied up to its banks. And while I'm still here I want privacy and security. I'm not likely to get that with you camping out in the reeds and thinking you can treat my island like your own garden, to visit whenever you feel like it,' he replied irascibly.

Catherine thought gloomily that it was just as well she hadn't mentioned the chickens or the vegetable plot.

'You wouldn't know I was there,' she persisted.

He looked her up and down. There was almost a dry amusement in his expression, although she doubted that his mouth cracked into a smile more than once a year.

'Don't you believe it,' he said, as cold as the Arctic. 'The answer's no. Get used to it.'

The cracked ice eyes tried to freeze her resolve over the rim of the mug. She'd never heard such a definite refusal in her life. But what did she have to lose?

'I can understand your reservations, but think of the advantages,' she coaxed, all soft sugar and reason. 'I could keep an eye on things while you're away—'

'Forget it,' he snapped, swallowing both pills with a gulp of coffee. 'I'll install an alarm system.'

She winced, imagining sirens wailing across the peaceful countryside and emptying it of animal life for ever.

'OK.' She sighed. 'Your position is clear. Nevertheless, I think I'll wait and see what your wife has to say,' she told him, playing her last, desperate card.

'You'll have a long wait,' he muttered.

She frowned. 'I don't see why. She's been here several times already. Everyone's seen her. She drives a yellow car and she supervised the men in the removal van—'

'Word does get about,' he drawled.

'That's because the removal men didn't get a tip,' she said tightly. 'They went into the local pub for a much-needed drink and complained that your wife was tight-fisted—considering they had to trudge across the bridge and through the orchard with everything you own!'

'I'll rectify that. But your gossips shouldn't jump to conclusions,' he shot back. 'She's my PA, not my wife. I'm divorced.'

Somehow she managed to stop herself from declaring that she wasn't surprised. Her fingers played with the handle on her mug. The woman with egg-whisk hair had been a long shot, but a possible ally, nevertheless. Now her last hope was gone. Her body slumped a little in the chair.

'There's no way I can persuade you to let me live here till the new owner takes over?' she begged in a small voice. 'You see, I'll lose my business if I can't work from my boat—'

'Wait a minute!' His frown was ferocious. 'I had the impression that you were asking to moor here *occasionally*. You're talking about a *permanent* arrangement?'

'Yes,' she admitted meekly. 'I've been here three years, you see. It would mean nothing to you, to let me tie up, but it would be everything to me. My whole livelihood would go if I have to leave. I have people who rely on me for regular—'

'That's your problem, not mine. I want you gone. See to it.'

Catherine rose to her feet, wondering what he would look like with half a pint of blackcurrant tea poured over his head. But dignity stayed her hand.

'Very well. I'll go,' she said coolly. 'But when it's known how you've treated me, it will be your problem, too.'

'Is that a threat?' he growled.

She shrugged. 'I just know what the local people are like. Treat them with courtesy and respect and they'll go to the ends of the earth for you. Treat them or their friends badly...' She shook her head as if he was making a huge mistake. 'I just hope your plumbing doesn't fail, or that you ever need help in the garden.'

And she stalked out before he could reply. Despite her bravado, she was shaking from the confrontation. And miserably she faced up to the fact that she was on the brink of leaving her beloved Tresanton Island for ever.

CHAPTER FIVE

EVEN as he followed her he knew he'd regret it. It would be far wiser to leave her to fly off in a huff and never see her again.

But of course, he argued, craning his neck to see where she'd gone, he had that bequest in the will to fulfil. And Catherine was the only person he knew who might tell him the whereabouts of the mysterious Perdita that Edith had mentioned.

Otherwise he wouldn't be ruining a perfectly good pair of shoes by plunging through dense undergrowth in the search for a tiny scrap of a woman who seemed to have got so thoroughly under his skin that he was still tingling from head to toe in places he didn't even know *could* tingle.

Wretched female! Irritably he pulled away a ferocious bramble which was trying to capture his jacket. He swore under his breath when it ripped the expensive cloth.

That was *it*. He'd had it up to here. She could take herself off and Perdita would have to do without the fifteen thousand pounds that Edith had left her—unless she read his advert, which he was honour bound to publish in the broadsheets.

He had work to do. Calls to make. This house was going to take up enough of his precious time, without him adding a stroppy flower child to his action list.

Fine. He'd made his decision.

And yet…he couldn't carry it out. He, Mr Decisive

himself. Something was holding him back. Curiosity, perhaps.

He grunted. Who was he kidding? *Catherine* was stopping him. A woman of extreme contradictions. Delicate and yet strong, sometimes laser-sharp with her eyes and tongue but with a voice so soft that it soothed his churning brain. A stubborn mouth. A smile that could melt diamonds.

Even more oddly, she was an old-fashioned sort of woman he wouldn't have looked at twice if she'd walked past him in London. He went for the elegant type, well-groomed, high maintenance. They looked good and knew how to work a room. Catherine wouldn't even know what that meant.

And yet his body had danced the moment he'd really looked at her. Flashes of intelligence and fire from those chocolate drop eyes had intrigued him. So had her face, seemingly fragile enough for the bones to be crushed if his hands ever cradled it. Not that they would, of course.

His mind skittered into thinking of her body. Lithe and flexible. Incredibly sensual despite its slimness...

No. This overwhelming urge to see her again was too ridiculous. He'd return to the house and...

He jumped as a chicken scuttled out of the bushes. Not an ordinary one—this was the size of a turkey and a kind of pinky buff. With a black beard, for heaven's sake. It saw him, stopped in surprise and came up to him with an almost hopeful look on its intelligent face.

Well, OK, he amended, feeling stupid. That bright-eyed, head on one side look *could* have been interpreted as intelligent.

'I suppose you're Edith's, too, are you?' he muttered, and looked around furtively, suddenly embarrassed at talking to a chicken.

He sighed. The poor thing must have been living on air. Unless Catherine had been feeding it. He wouldn't put it past her.

The chicken began to unpick his shoelace and he hurriedly moved on, heading back to the house. His steps were annoyingly reluctant, but he had far too much to do to chase after Catherine.

She'd soon go. And if she didn't, he'd get the lawyers on to her. Any chickens would have to be sold or killed for the nearest market. Problem solved. He'd put Jane on to that one and keep her out of mischief, he thought with relief.

Once indoors, he went upstairs to find the master bedroom. He wasn't interested in anywhere else, only where he'd sleep. There wasn't time for aimless wandering.

Jane had hung up his suits and stored the rest of his clothes with unnerving care. He checked that he had everything he needed and settled down at the desk in the window, where she'd placed his computer.

Waiting for it to power up, he wriggled out of his jacket, slipped it over the back of the chair and happened to glance idly at the view of the garden.

He was high enough to see to the end of the island. A branch of the path ran from the bridge to the far side, though its destination was concealed by huge rhododendrons, their buds fat and ready to burst.

He froze. A man in a red T-shirt and jeans was walking along the path towards the rhododendrons. Zach's scowl deepened. One of Catherine's friends, no doubt.

Hopefully he'd find she'd gone and wouldn't trespass on his land again. If he had any trouble, he'd have to put a locked gate on the bridge. This was his land, not a public park!

Angrily he punched in his password and concentrated

on the day's prices. Or tried to. Over the next hour he kept looking up, drawn by the view. Extraordinarily, the more he did, the more he felt his muscles relax.

The tension had eased from his shoulders. His muscles felt liquid instead of rock hard. And his almost permanent headache had cleared.

There must be something restful about the garden. He pursed his lips and tried to work out what it might be. Those soft, harmonising colours, perhaps? The variety of shapes—tall, conical trees and shrubs, weeping ones, fat, exuberant ones and some with feathery leaves? It was really rather attractive, he had to admit—

He held his breath, his smug serenity suddenly shattered. The intruder was on his way back, making for the bridge. On his way he passed a second man, who nodded as if they were both strangers to one another. This new arrival walked on steadily towards the rhododendrons. And, presumably, Catherine.

Bristling with indignation, he was thundering down the stairs before he knew it. Thrusting his feet into his mud-caked shoes. Hurrying in the direction of those damn rhododendrons. This was his land. *His.*

And these men... She'd talked about people who needed her. That she'd lose her livelihood if her regulars...

His breath came short in his throat as he thought the unthinkable. Surely she wasn't...a *prostitute*?

Immediately as the idea came into his head he dismissed it out of hand. She seemed too innocent and unworldly. But the thought lingered, nevertheless. And he wondered grimly what he'd find.

He reached the end of the path, giant hens scattering before him, and studied the brightly painted boat snuggling up to the bank. It was half-hidden by overhanging trees, with just the bow and stern visible.

The entire boat seemed to be rocking gently. His jaw tightened and he had to force himself not to listen to the evil voice in his head that was telling him *why* it might be rocking. Only one way to find out.

Gingerly he stepped down on to the blue-painted deck. There was a notice which had been hung on the brass handles of the brightly coloured cabin doors. 'Hello! Welcome. Please wait outside,' it said. Naturally he ignored it and pushed the doors open.

Catherine looked up in surprise as Zach's bulk filled the doorway. Immediately she noticed his fury. And took charge before he let rip with his mercurial temper.

'I'm working,' she declared with firm authority. 'Please go outside and wait until I've finished.'

There was a breathless moment while their eyes clashed and she recognised utter contempt in his expression.

'*Working*?' he spat out, with a fearsome glare at her virtually naked client.

'As you see. I'll be half an hour at least,' she replied tightly.

With a snort of disgust he withdrew, slamming the doors behind him.

'I'm sorry about that. Landlord trouble,' she said ruefully to Joe.

'That's OK,' he murmured in a dreamy haze, his senses spinning from her expert hands.

She began to work her magic again but it took her a while to become properly focused. Instead of concentrating on Joe's needs her mind kept wandering off to think about Zach. *Now* what had she done to annoy him? He really was the most irascible of men!

Forty minutes later she had waved goodbye to yet another satisfied client and was tucking away the cash he'd given her when Zach came in, clambering awkwardly down the narrow wooden steps into the cabin.

He frowned at the notes in her hand. Tight-lipped, Catherine closed the lid of her cash box, locked it, and then folded away the drop-down bed where Joe had been lying. It took that long for her to gain total control of her temper.

'If you're wondering why I haven't gone yet...' she began haughtily.

'Why didn't you tell me you're operating a floating brothel?' he demanded savagely.

'A...?'

Blank amazement turned swiftly to a smile. Which became a broad grin and finally outright laughter.

She was almost hysterical from laughing by the time he caught her arms and gave her a brief shake.

'It's not funny!' he snarled. 'I suppose circumstances have driven you to whoring, but—'

'I'm not a prostitute,' she gasped out, wiping her streaming eyes. 'Really, Zach! I haven't even got the right clothes! There isn't a pair of fishnet tights in sight! And you may not have noticed, but we're horribly short of street corners here!'

His mouth was thin with disbelief. 'I saw a steady stream of men—'

'Two, I think,' she answered drily.

'All right!' he snapped, far angrier than seemed necessary. 'Two to my knowledge and goodness knows how many more lined up on the bank waiting for their turn!' he hurled.

'Don't be ridiculous—!' she gasped.

'I know what I saw! That last one was stripped naked on your bed and you were bending over him, your hands

doing heaven knows what when I opened those doors!'
he stormed. 'If that isn't evidence, I don't know what is!
How dare you use my island as a knocking shop? I suppose you pulled the wool over Edith's eyes about your
activities, but you won't find me so naïve!'

He didn't want to listen to her, that was clear. She
shrugged and slid from his grasp. What did she care if he
thought badly of her? He wasn't worth the effort of explaining.

'Is that why you came here?' she asked with a sigh.

'You bet it was!' he spat. 'You've got to get out of
here. Now! I won't have this going on under my nose—'
He broke off with an irritable mutter when his phone
played an incongruously merry tune. 'Damn! Thought I'd
turned that off!' he growled.

Staring angrily at the display, he evidently decided the
caller was important because he answered with a suddenly
gentle 'Hello.'

Giving him up as a bad job, Catherine turned away.
She was now resigned to leaving in the next two minutes,
so she began to check her appointments to see who she'd
have to cancel.

Perhaps, she mused, she could risk taking a temporary
mooring nearer to the village. But she'd have to keep
moving every two weeks, that was the law. It didn't bode
well for a thriving business.

Without realising it, she found herself listening to
Zach's conversation. It sounded as if he'd turned into another person altogether. He was speaking warmly, even
lovingly. And for such a positive, dogmatic man he
seemed strangely anxious.

'You see,' he was saying carefully, 'the house isn't
what I expected. It's quite unsuitable... Because it's on an
island...yes... Well, I suppose it is exciting... You have

to cross over a bridge... No. Narrow. Wooden—like the ones in adventure stories...'

Intrigued, she slanted a quick glance at Zach. He looked astonished, as if he hadn't expected the caller to be interested in his purchase. Was this his ex-wife? Girlfriend?

'But it's nowhere near any cinema, or a burger bar...' he cautioned and she knew he must be speaking to a child. 'Boats? Er...yes, there are boats, but I wouldn't know if...' There was a long pause while Zach listened intently, his face clearing as if the sun had come out. 'Of course I'll try. Leave it to me. See you tomorrow, Sam,' he said huskily. 'OK. Early, providing that's all right with your mother,' he agreed, suddenly elated. 'Yes. I know it'll be just for the Saturday. She told me about your party on Sunday. I understand. Look forward to seeing you.'

He couldn't believe it. Sam actually wanted to visit! Though, he thought ruefully, it was undoubtedly the island and its bridge that had appealed. Still, it was a start.

How long Sam's interest would last, he didn't know. But there might be an hour or two when the two of them didn't behave as if a wall of ice lay between them.

Smiling, he caught Catherine's enquiring eye. 'My son,' he said lovingly, wanting to share his delight. 'Coming for the day.'

'He'll have a whale of a time,' she replied softly.

'Do you think? Doing what?' Zach looked perplexed.

'A million things. He could build a camp from branches and stuff. Bully you into making him a tree house. His imagination can run riot here. Play pirates, Treasure Island... Oh, it's the place of boys' dreams.'

It was? Maybe she was right. Slowly he nodded, seeing the possibilities. And suddenly with the rush of pleasure that maybe this wouldn't turn out to be a disaster after all, he felt unusually generous.

'Look,' he said gruffly. 'I appreciate the fact that you have to earn your living any way you can. And I know it's going to be difficult for you to move.' He reached in his back pocket and lifted out his wallet, unaware of her look of horror. Peeling off a stack of fifties, he held them out, his conscience satisfied. 'Here. To help you settle somewhere else.'

She stepped back, her eyes showing her hurt. 'No, thank you,' she said curtly.

'Go on!' he encouraged. 'You must need it—'

'No,' she said with dignity. 'I don't need it any more than I need your patronising gestures. Perhaps you'd go and leave me to stow away my stuff. I have to find somewhere else to tie up before dusk falls.'

'You're a stubborn woman,' he muttered, astonished that she should refuse so much money.

She seemed to draw herself to her full height. Touchingly, she was still only as tall as his chest.

'One day,' she said quietly, 'you'll learn that there's more to life than money. People like to feel good about themselves. Integrity matters to my well-being.'

'Integrity?' he spluttered.

'Yes. Would you leave, please? You're trespassing on my boat.'

Now he was *trespassing*? He couldn't believe her nerve! His teeth jammed together in anger. And he swung abruptly on his heel, storming out of the narrow boat and back to the house, quite unreasonably disturbed by the value Catherine set on her honour.

After all, she was no better than she should be.

He made a hash of his deals that afternoon. And as the evening drew on, he found he wasn't even able to take in the figures on his spread sheets—figures that were usually child's play to him.

Infuriatingly, his head was full of her. Blazing brown eyes, full of scorn. Soft mouth suddenly scornful and quivering with righteous indignation. Supple body rigid with anger. And pride. Such pride—despite her chosen way of life!

He sobered. Perhaps it was all she had left, the only thing that held her self-respect together. Although he hated what she was doing, he felt a grudging admiration for her. He'd never met anyone like Catherine. And probably never would.

Though it was just as well. In her profession, she needed to know how to lure men and make them desire her. She'd certainly hit all the right buttons where he was concerned. He shifted in his seat to dissipate the ache in his loins.

Sternly he told himself that her sultry looks were part of an act. And, he thought in disgust, he didn't want to get involved in her sexual games. She was only interested in one thing; permission to keep her floating whorehouse tied up to his island.

Strangely depressed, despite the prospect of his son's arrival the next day, he went down to the kitchen, found an instant meal and pushed it in the microwave.

Eating its tasteless contents in the silent house, he found himself thinking of Catherine and the good friends she'd talked about. Much to his surprise, he wondered how she would fare without them since they meant so much to her.

Slowly he returned to his desk upstairs, his feet ponderous and leaden as he approached the window.

And held his breath. The black, moonless night was punctured by tiny white fairy lights which bedecked the path leading to Catherine's boat. It was a beautiful sight.

He opened the window. Somewhere a set of wooden wind chimes played tunes with the breeze. He became aware that unfamiliar and delicious scents were assailing his nostrils.

For a long time he stood there, just letting the night air and its strange sounds wash over him. New York awaited his call, but he was reluctant to tear himself away. Instead, he leant over the windowsill, intent on the extraordinarily liquid notes of a bird.

Didn't birds stop singing when it got dark? Suddenly alert with pleasure, he realised it must be a nightingale. The first he'd ever heard. And, yes, it was a lyrical and joyous song. He felt privileged, as if he'd been awarded a great prize.

Disappointingly, it stopped. With a faint smile of regret, he was about to close the window when he heard voices. Beams of light swept the path and soon he could make out a group of young men, hurrying along with bottles tucked under their arms. After a short time a larger crowd followed; men, women and children, bearing what was clearly plates of food.

His face darkened. She was still there, then!

'Catherine's friends,' he mused, irritated that she'd ignored his order to leave.

Presumably this mixed bunch of people were saying goodbye to her. His brows drew together. They didn't seem to care what she was.

He thought with some distaste of the naked man on her bed. Of Catherine's pliable body, intent on serving her client's needs. His lip curled. And they said that cities were a hotbed of immorality!

Grimly he pushed aside the fact that really bothered him. It had been Catherine who was offering her body so freely, Catherine who spent her working hours pretending to men that she enjoyed their clumsy fumblings. And he couldn't handle his feelings on that score.

What really annoyed him was that initially she'd lied; assuming indignation and protesting her innocence. But in the end she'd been unable to deny his accusations— though he'd half-hoped he'd made a mistake and there would be a simple explanation.

Whatever the case, he wouldn't be made a fool of. If she hadn't gone by the morning, he decided irascibly, he'd damn well cut her adrift.

CHAPTER SIX

JUST after dawn Catherine rolled sleepily from her bed, showered and dressed then scattered grain about to encourage the chickens into the assorted cat baskets which she'd borrowed.

Her own breakfast would have to be taken on the run. When she had tried to start her engine the previous afternoon it had spluttered and died and no amount of coaxing would persuade it back into life again.

Still, it had been an ill wind. At least she'd been able to say goodbye to her friends. She gave a wan smile. So much laughter, so many tears…

Things to do, she told herself briskly. And, slipping a pair of overalls on top of her shorts and T-shirt, she grabbed her tool kit from a locker and removed the lock and chain on the engine hole hatch in the stern. There followed a good two hours of frustration, during which she became daubed in oil and grease.

'Wow!'

Catherine lifted her head from the bowels of the engine, her face flushed from exertion. She looked to see who'd spoken.

'Hello,' she said, smiling broadly at the skinny little boy.

Sam, she thought immediately. Let out loose to play while Daddy fixed his mobile to his ear and flung orders into the ether.

And her heart softened at the sight of the kiddie. He was pale and entirely lacking in his father's air of confidence. He stood on the bank, smoky grey eyes wide with fascination, his body language revealing an intense shyness that was battling with an equally intense curiosity.

'Those your chickens?' he asked in awe, nodding at her Silver Laced hens.

'That's right.' Fondly she eyed her tiny chickens eating their way towards the baskets. Next to her huge Faverolles they looked very dainty with every white feather delicately edged in black. She jumped on to the bank, shooed some in and fastened the clasps. 'These big ones are mine, too. They come from France.'

'Mega!' he declared. Nervously he stretched out a hand to a fat buff hen nearby. An expression of delight spread over his face. 'It's letting me stroke it! Oh! It feels all soft and warm!'

Picking up a stray and giving it a fond stroke, she nodded in a friendly way.

'They're very tame. They have pink eggs, you know.'

'Yuk! Girly!' He grinned, disarmed.

'Like to help me get the hens into their baskets?' she asked.

'Would I!'

They worked for a few moments, shooing in the last stragglers, and she fastened the clasps. She boarded the boat. Struggling with the weight of the baskets, Sam passed them to her and she placed them securely on the cabin roof.

'Six...seven, eight,' she counted. 'All the Silver Laced present and correct. Four Favs. Good! Thanks a lot,' she said cheerfully. 'Now I can go back to that engine.'

Sam craned his neck to see. 'What are you doing with it?'

'Trying to get it to start,' she answered with a rueful

grin. Then on a sudden impulse, she added; 'Want to help?'

'Ohhh! Can I?' gasped Sam, squeezing just about every excited muscle in his small person.

'Of course. Come on board. Take my hand.'

'Oh, cool!' Jumping eagerly on to the deck, he peered into the engine hole with wide-eyed fascination. 'What can I do?'

Dubiously she considered his pale blue shirt and beige shorts. They had been ironed within an inch of their lives, the knife-edge creases in danger of slashing any passing stranger. She wondered if he'd actually dared to sit down yet.

'You'll get dirty unless we find something for you to wear,' she observed.

Shining eyes turned to her, eyes that oddly reminded her of his father. Although Sam's coaxed and Zach's eyes commanded, she thought, returning a few moments later with an old T-shirt of hers and a couple of bulldog clips.

'There!' she declared with satisfaction when she'd covered him up from neck to knee.

He didn't seem to mind having the clips sitting perkily on his bony shoulders. At least they'd taken up the slack, and now he could forage to his heart's content.

'Right,' she said cheerfully. 'Pass me that spanner, please.'

'Spanner.'

She hid a grin. Sam had obviously watched hospital soaps.

'Rag.' She held out her hand, surgeon-like.

'Rag,' Sam said solemnly and to her delight it was slapped into her hand in the manner of a theatre nurse.

'Oil.' There was a pause. Surfacing, she saw that he was looking doubtfully at the array of cans in her engine box. She dived down again. 'One can, complete with little spout,' she expanded.

The oil was smacked into her hand and a small, confiding head came down to hers, breathing pure joy.

'I've never worked on an engine before!' Sam sighed blissfully.

'Couldn't have done this without you,' she fibbed. 'Finger there, please,' she said, choosing somewhere he could do no harm. 'Hold it absolutely steady...'

'My dad knows about boats,' Sam whispered in her ear, his finger going an alarming shade of white.

Probably the market value of an oil tanker, she thought uncharitably.

'*Does* he?' she replied, injecting a totally unfelt admiration for the child's sake. 'Lift that finger a fraction...'

'Grandpa had a barge on the Thames,' Sam said surprisingly.

'Good grief!'

She jerked her head around to stare at the small, solemn face close to hers. Who would have thought it? She'd imagined Zach had been born in a pin-stripe romper suit with a silver mobile hooked over his ear. It seemed he was the son of an ordinary mortal after all!

'Perhaps we should ask your father to stick his head down here and sort us out,' she joked.

'I could go and ask him!' Sam cried excitedly.

'No! Er...I'm sure he's busy—'

'Yeah. He's always busy,' Sam confided in a forlorn voice.

Catherine winced. And silently cursed Zach for being ignorant of the important things in life.

'No problem,' she declared cheerily. 'We'll get this done, you and me.'

Sam's chest swelled with pride. 'Then we can show him!' he cried.

Poor kiddie. He was desperate to impress his unimpressable father.

'He'll be amazed,' she promised, vowing that she'd make darn sure that he was.

'Cool!' breathed Sam with a blissful smile.

She handed him back the spanner and noticed that somehow he'd already managed to get himself covered in oil.

'Uh-oh! We are going to be in the most awful trouble unless we pop you in my shower before you go back,' she said with a giggle. 'Your face is black. And look at your hands!'

'You're all oily too!' laughed Sam. 'It's all over your forehead and cheeks—'

'*Sam!* What on earth—?'

They eyed one another, startled. Sam looked horribly like a rabbit trapped in headlights. Slowly they straightened and they both turned to look at the tight-lipped Zach on the bank.

She giggled at the picture they must present and grabbed Sam's trembling hand and swung it backwards and forwards to reassure him.

At least, she thought, Zach was more sensibly dressed for island life. Apart from his annoying X factor that made her heart bump uncomfortably, he could have been almost normal in jeans, a cream polo shirt and muddied loafers. Pity about his wall-to-wall frown, though.

'Sam! You're filthy!' he exclaimed in reproval. 'And what *do* you think you look like in that outfit?'

His son stiffened, glanced down at the T-shirt and squirmed beside the furious Catherine.

'No problem. The oil's not permanent. It'll wash off,'

she dismissed, remaining sweet and modulated for Sam's sake. 'And this is his makeshift overall. We thought you'd rather his clothes weren't spoilt. I do hope that was the right decision.' Her wide eyes, all innocence, fixed on the annoyed Zach. 'Sam's been helping me to mend my engine. And good morning to you, Zachariah,' she added drily.

The frown had intensified at her use of his full name.

'*You* are not supposed to be here,' he snapped, while his son shifted uncomfortably from one foot to the other.

Catherine gently squeezed Sam's hand and gave him a huge smile. It didn't come easily. She wanted to scowl back at Zach and tear strips off him.

'I know,' she agreed as equably as possible.

'Then why are you still hanging around?' Zach demanded in an irritable growl.

Ruefully she looked down at her oily overalls.

'You're good at putting two and two together, I understand. I leave you to guess.'

With a grunt of exasperation, he came closer to the edge of the bank and peered at the engine hole.

'Engine trouble? You could have checked it over yesterday,' he reproved.

'I did,' she replied meekly. 'I fiddled about for ages till it got too dark to work.'

'And then you had a party.'

It sounded as if she'd recklessly opened an opium den.

'My friends gave me a farewell do,' she corrected.

Zach grunted and glanced sourly around, giving the impression he was searching for hypodermics and perhaps even a few stray revellers.

'Hmm. I must say, I expected to find the place strewn with beer cans and bottles,' he muttered.

'Heavens! We're more civilised than that. Were you

spying on me?' she countered in an amiable tone, conscious that Sam was looking up at her with a kind of scared admiration. She doubted that many people stood up to his father.

Slightly embarrassed, Zach thrust his hands into his jeans pockets. 'Of course not! My desk is in a bedroom window,' he replied curtly. 'I could hardly miss the procession beating *my* path to your door. I certainly couldn't avoid hearing everyone going home.'

She grinned, remembering the affectionate farewells, the exchanges of phone numbers and addresses. She'd had no idea so many people in the village were so fond of her. It had been a fabulous send-off.

Feeling generous, she beamed at the cold-hearted City man whose life probably lacked such riches.

'Sorry if we disturbed you,' she said with genuine warmth. 'They all promised they wouldn't sing on the way back.'

'They didn't,' Zach conceded gruffly. 'It was just…the murmur of voices. Laughter. I happened to be still working.'

At two in the morning? she thought in amazement.

'Good. They didn't wake you then,' she said, thinking that she'd won that one. 'And you can be sure that it won't happen again, can't you?' she added with a sad sigh.

'That's right. It won't.' He turned his attention to his son, who was clutching Catherine's hand tightly. 'Sam, you haven't had your breakfast. And I told you the river was dangerous,' he scolded.

'Sorry, Dad. You were on the phone,' Sam explained meekly. 'I went for an explore.'

He had the grace to colour up. 'I got involved. Something very important.'

'Yes, Dad.'

Poor child! she thought. To be ignored for some wretched business call—it was unforgivable. No wonder the kiddie looked crushed.

'You must do your exploring with me,' Zach told him firmly. 'Now, Miss Leigh has things to do. Come off that boat.'

Her hand closed around the scrawny shoulder.

'Can't he—?' she began.

'No. Let go of my son!' he ordered.

She sensed the little boy's deflation and wanted to give him a hug, but he'd already taken his father's outstretched hand and jumped to the bank.

'What a shame. I enjoyed having him with me. You're acting as if I'm contagious,' she complained, annoyed at the kiddie's scurrying obedience. The poor child looked miserable.

'Your morals might be,' Zach muttered.

'So that's it!' she exclaimed indignantly. 'I'd forgotten! Just a moment. Wait there. I'll show you!'

Grim-lipped, she hurried into the cabin and grabbed her framed diplomas from their hooks. She dearly wanted to spend a little more time with the sweet-natured Sam. But she knew that Zach would frown on that if he thought she was hell bent on corrupting a minor by introducing him into a world of pimps and prostitutes.

'Here,' she said in a tone of injured pride, after stepping on to the bank and presenting Zach with her precious diplomas. 'I think these will relieve your anxiety about your child's moral welfare.'

When he glanced at the first one his cold expression became even chillier. 'A masseuse?' he muttered, giving her an old-fashioned look.

'It's not what you're thinking,' she said tartly. 'I'm

fully qualified from a respectable society, as you see. Therapeutic and Sports Massage does wonders for muscle injuries. And it works miracles on muscle tension in stressed-out people too,' she added meaningfully.

'I bet,' he muttered, and she went hot beneath his dark and mocking glance. Cynically he examined the rest of the framed certificates. And did a double-take. '*Homoeopath?* You?' he said in surprise.

'Height isn't a requirement,' she quipped.

'Evidently,' he drawled, but seemed faintly amused because his mouth had quivered a fraction. Though nothing as revolutionary as a real smile.

'What's a homey-thing, Daddy?' asked Sam, his eyebrows drawn together in an exact copy of his father's.

Seeing Zach's look of uncertainty, she crouched down and took Sam's small hands in hers.

'Ho-me-oh-path,' she said softly. 'That means I've studied in a college in London. I help people when they're ill,' she explained.

'Like a doctor?' Sam asked, wide-eyed.

'Kind of,' she conceded. 'But my medicines trigger the body to heal itself. They're made only from natural things, like plants and minerals and so on. If you were bitten by an adder, for instance, I'd give you a tiny, watered-down dose of Vipera, which is made from the adder's poison.'

'Wow!' Sam breathed, his eyes now like saucers. 'Anything else weird you give people?'

Amused, she tried to think of something he'd recognise. It was difficult simplifying a method of treatment that was so complex and comprehensive.

'Well, supposing you couldn't sleep, night after night because your mind was churning with thoughts—'

'Like it does on Christmas Eve, or just before a birthday?' broke in Sam eagerly.

'That's it!' she approved, and was rewarded by his pleased smile. 'Then I might use a medicine made from coffee beans.'

'Coffee keeps you awake,' objected Zach scornfully.

'Exactly.' She stood up, her face betraying the passion she felt for her profession. 'That's how homoeopathy works. What harms you, cures you in tiny doses. Take the bark of the Cinchona tree. It can cause violent fevers. Even conventional medicine uses it to cure malaria—'

'No. They use quinine,' Zach broke in with an expression of contempt.

'Cinchona *is* quinine,' she replied.

'Hippocrates would be turning in his grave,' he dismissed.

'Hippocrates,' she said, sticking up for the Father of Medicine's incredible genius, 'believed that what caused illness could cure it.'

Zach grunted. 'I'll stick to conventional medicine, thanks.'

'I wasn't trying to convert you,' she said drily. 'Only to reassure you about my morals.'

He pursed his lips, considering her thoughtfully.

'Those men I saw... They were your patients, I suppose.'

'That's right,' she answered gravely.

'Only men?' he shot back.

She sighed. He was hard to convince of her integrity.

'No. I also treat children, women, and old ladies. And babies. They're my speciality. If you step inside I could show you the book which lists my patients and the remedies they've had. And they and many others are going to miss me when I go, because we're half-way through their treatments.'

The frown cleared and her heart did its fatal *bump*.

'I apologise,' he said and drew in a deep breath. 'Whatever I think of your crazy medical ideas, I admit I maligned you.' He looked faintly embarrassed. 'I don't usually jump to conclusions like that. But…I'd seen you and that man with my own eyes and—'

'It's OK,' she said, unable to take the breath-stopping effect of his soft gaze any longer. 'It must have looked bad,' she added generously.

'It did.' He scowled. 'And you didn't do anything to dispel my assumption.'

'As I recall, you weren't in a mood to listen,' she pointed out.

'Hmph. You could be right. Forgive me?' he asked shortly, holding out his hand.

It wasn't the most gracious of apologies but it was all she was being offered. And something told her that this had been a huge concession on Zach's part and that he rarely admitted he might be wrong.

She looked at the outstretched hand. 'Forgiven,' she agreed.

And, with a smile, she took it. A sensation of protective warmth flooded through her and for one mad moment she wanted to stay linked to him like that for ever.

But abruptly his grip relaxed and he drew his hand away with a slightly insulting rapidity that suggested he objected to physical contact with her.

'You promised me a shower on your boat,' Sam reminded her anxiously, bringing her back to earth.

'We've got our own—' Zach began stiffly.

'I promised,' she told him gently, sad to see the forlorn little boy standing four chilly inches from his father. 'And you wouldn't want his mucky fingers all over the house, would you?' An urge to do something, to make a difference to this dysfunctional father and son, swept recklessly over her. 'Look, I'm starving and you haven't had break-fast.' She grinned at Sam's hopeful face. 'Why don't we mechanics get cleaned up and cook something nourish-ing?' she suggested.

'Me? Cook?' he squeaked.

'Why not? I've got new-laid eggs, still warm from the hens—'

'*Pink* ones?' Sam breathed.

'You don't get pink eggs...' began Zach.

'Oh, yes, you do,' she said with a laugh. 'Wait till you see them. And we'll have home-made bread, herby sau-sages, mushrooms and tomatoes. How's that sound?'

'Oh!' breathed Sam, suddenly in ecstasy again. 'I'd love to cook. *And* eat on a boat! Could I, Dad?' he asked timidly. He put his small hands together in an earnest entreaty. 'Please, *please*?'

Zach cleared his throat, peculiarly moved. He'd never known his son so excited. He was reminded of his own uncontainable joy when he'd first stood proudly on his father's barge at the age of six. He had chugged down the Thames in a haze of delight.

They'd eaten doorstep sandwiches of cheese and ham and never had food tasted so good. People had waved at them and his father had pointed out places of interest. For a whole day he'd been close to his father and even now he could remember the rush of disappointment when it was time to go home.

Ruthlessly he tucked away that memory. It was making him feel sentimental. But suddenly his stomach seemed desperate for a cooked breakfast. It had sounded mouth-watering the way Catherine had described it.

His son looked up at him trustingly, the habitual ex-pression of uncertainty suddenly replaced by a huge grin as he recognised capitulation when he saw it.

'Dad?' Sam prompted in a hushed whisper.

Zach's heart turned over. How he loved his child! And Catherine and her boat were providing him with a means to break down the barriers that had frozen the ground between him and Sam. It wouldn't hurt. She'd be gone in a few hours.

'Why not? Catherine,' he said decisively, 'thank you for your invitation. We accept.'

'Whoopee! Thanks, Dad!' squealed Sam, flinging his arms around Zach's knees.

He melted from head to toe. *Contact!* he thought. At last. After all these years of avoidance...

'Thank Catherine,' he prompted huskily.

'Yes! Thanks a million, trillion!' cried Sam, jumping up and down.

She laughed. 'You haven't tasted my cooking yet,' she warned with a giggle. 'Now. How about we whip off that T-shirt here, and get you into that shower? Then after breakfast, if it's OK with your father and you don't have any other plans, I'll show you around the boat. After that, I really must get back to sorting out my engine.'

Zach felt oddly elated as they scrambled on board and she led them into the rear cabin which she called the boatman's cabin. It was small and neat and Sam lingered in awe, asking a flood of questions. Zach couldn't relate this to the reserved, reticent child he'd been struggling to communicate with.

But Sam had been different from the moment his mother had dropped him off by the river. He'd never shown any interest in boats or the country before, but the island and the bridge had totally captured his interest.

To his amusement and Kate's Sam had run backwards and forwards over the wooden structure with such joy on his face that it had physically hurt Zach.

And now he could feel the contentment emanating from his son, even when Catherine firmly insisted that he should clean himself up first and that they'd have to leave the Grand Tour till after breakfast.

He watched her talking easily to Sam, clasping his son's hand as if they'd been friends for years.

Zach sympathised. She had that effect on him too. That morning, when he'd first seen that the boat was still there, he'd felt a totally irrational surge of pleasure which had mentally knocked him off balance. That was why he'd been so angry. He didn't do 'irrational'.

But something akin to tenderness had touched his heart when she'd turned to face him like a guilty child, oil-streaked and apologetic. And then, he had to admit, he had been stricken with jealousy.

Sam had obviously been having a good time. It had hurt that his son had been so reluctant to leave her. Thoughtfully he followed the small figures along a corridor into a tiny bathroom.

'Here,' he said gruffly. 'I'll unbutton your shirt, Sam. Your fingers are too mucky.'

He crouched down. Obediently his son stood, happily watching Catherine as she bustled about with towels and tested the setting on the shower.

It had been a long time since he'd undressed Sam. In fact, his son had shied away from physical contact of any kind and had made it quite plain that affectionate gestures on Zach's part were distinctly unwelcome.

'Give it time,' his ex-wife had said sympathetically. 'He's hurting from our break-up. Perhaps he wants to punish you.'

Punish! He winced. It had been three years of torture. Zach had given his son some space. Great wide gaps of it. And their perfunctory, dutiful kisses had torn the heart from him.

'There you go,' he said unnecessarily.

'Thanks, Dad.'

That had been accompanied by a huge and happy smile which made him want to weep. He felt a huge lurch of love at the frailty of the small bones and the innocence in those soft grey eyes as his child waited patiently in his underwear for the adventure to continue.

Thank you, Catherine, he thought fervently. Thank you for this chance to find my son. The child I love above all else.

'All set, Sam. Now, would you like to know a special rule of this boat?' Catherine asked when she'd explained to Sam how to turn on the shower.

Zach rose to his feet, admiring her technique. Sam was putty in her hands, his proud 'Yes, please!' indicating that he'd do anything for her.

'Right. Of course, I'm sure you know already that water is precious,' she said in her gentle voice. 'But on a boat every drop counts because it isn't piped into our homes as it is in your house.'

'How do you get it then, if it doesn't come out of taps?' Sam wrinkled his forehead and Zach recognised his own frown on his son's small, perplexed face.

'We're lucky here. There's a tap with a hose on the bank which the previous owner had put in, so I can fill my tanks from that.'

'Where are the tanks?' Zach asked with interest.

'Under the fore deck, with an access point via the gas hatch,' she explained, looking up at him briefly.

'Gas? Is that…safe?' he asked, wondering why he felt so churned up by her dark glance. Their eyes seemed to lock and he felt a warmth stealing through his body.

'Propane,' she said huskily. 'It doesn't freeze.'

'Interesting,' he murmured.

To his surprise, she went a delicate shade of pink and turned back to Sam.

'On other moorings,' she went on hurriedly, 'sometimes we just have to take our boats along the river to fill up from one of the Water Authority's sites. They give us keys for that. So we get into the habit of using enough water to get clean, but no more. We don't hang about in the shower. Just get in, scrub madly and turn it off again. OK?'

Wryly Zach reckoned that it would have been OK if she'd suggested Sam rubbed himself with a scouring pad and coarse salt.

'Use a smear of this on the worst bits,' she instructed, taking off the lid of a small tin. 'The stuff in here will lift off the oil and grease. Then lather up as usual.'

With a warm smile, she closed a sliding door that shut off the shower area from the rest of the small bathroom and began to undo her overall straps. Feeling a little awkward, he hung around in the doorway waiting to help dry Sam when he came out.

The breath came short and rapid in his throat as she emerged like a butterfly from a cocoon, her brief cut-off shorts a kingfisher blue, her T-shirt clinging damply to her body. Her legs were fabulous; slender and toned and the colour of pale honey.

A bolt of electricity seemed to shoot across the room at him. He sucked in his stomach, taken aback by its unexpectedness. Why her? he marvelled, steeling himself to damp down the fires licking through his body.

She wasn't his sort. Too small. Too dark. Scornful of fashion and devoted to some airy-fairy medicine.

And yet...she was moving now as if drugged, her

graceful arms hanging up the overall on a peg as though she were performing in a ballet. Her slim body was so supple and…touchable that it was all he could do not to reach out and span that small waist with his hands. And then to run them around the curve of her spine and the…

'Zach,' she breathed, staring at him pink-faced again and pursing unnervingly kissable lips.

He dragged his hot gaze up to meet her startled eyes.

'Uh?' he grunted stupidly.

'Would you forage in the kitchen?' she asked breathily.

His brain seemed paralysed. His voice box had joined in too.

'What?' he forced out after a moment.

'There's…' She swallowed and he realised he must be staring too hard so he scowled at the wood block floor instead. 'There's a table flap that unhooks, er…knives, forks and plates, mugs and salt and pepper to find,' she finished in a rush.

'I was going to help Sam get dry,' he growled, feeling parched in the throat himself.

'Pop back in a moment. I'm going to wash,' she said hastily, turning her back on him and giving an odd kind of laugh. 'You must think I've met an oil slick head on.'

Fortunately she had no idea how appealing she looked and how badly he wanted to rub the smudge of black from her small nose. For absolutely no reason at all, he found himself chuckling softly under his breath.

She confounded him by jerking her head around in surprise. His hand lifted before he could stop it, and suddenly he didn't care. Mesmerised, she watched as his finger came her way and traced the path of that oil slick all the way across her smooth, flawless forehead and down her prominent cheekbones to the delicate jaw.

'Don't be long,' he muttered, finding it hard not to kiss her sweet mouth.

There was a crazy voice inside him, saying *why not do it*? even though his child was singing lustily a foot or so away. Coming to his senses, he recoiled, appalled by his behaviour.

She gulped. 'Why not?'

He managed to frown. 'Because I want to make sure Sam dries between his toes,' he snapped prosaically.

And before she could tempt him any more with that artless pink mouth he closed the door behind him.

He indulged in some deep breathing, spending a moment or two getting his brains back into his head.

OK. She was delectable. Unusual. Like no other woman he'd ever met. But that didn't mean he had to make a pass at her while his son was so close. Totally out of order.

Grimly he strode through the boat. Unlike him, it was in an immaculate state with nothing out of place at all. There were cupboards and gleaming brass everywhere and a general air of…cosiness. Armchairs invited him to lounge. Comfort seemed to surround him and unravel his irritation.

A little nonplussed by his sensation of ease in such alien surroundings, he passed by a huge bookshelf which lined the fore cabin wall.

In the Shaker-style kitchen beyond he found the drop-down table and everything Catherine had requested. He was about to return when she and Sam appeared, their faces glowing, identical great grins stretching from ear to ear.

'He did between his toes,' Catherine offered, giving Sam a friendly hug. And it was enthusiastically returned.

He felt extraordinarily helpless. This complete stranger

had effortlessly infused his son with joy and contentment. Something all his money and lavish gifts had failed to do.

He's my son, he thought bleakly. And I don't know how to win his love.

CHAPTER SEVEN

UNUSUALLY subdued, he watched Catherine and Sam bustling around preparing breakfast. His own pathetic attempts to slice mushrooms had resulted in half of them skittering to the floor.

Catherine pretended that this had been an accident, caused by the fact that there wasn't enough room for them all to do jobs.

'Why don't you relax?' she suggested gently. 'You could do the washing up afterwards.'

'I'm good at that,' he said with a grateful smile.

She could have made fun of his efforts. Most women would, in that amused and patronising voice they adopted when men strayed into areas they couldn't handle.

So he lounged back on the bench cushions, increasingly fascinated by the length and slenderness of her neck, and the way that strands of her amazing hair tumbled in silken coils from the huge gold clip on top of her head.

Deft and willowy, she worked with an economy of movement borne of necessity in the cramped kitchen. And her soft, murmuring voice soothed him, lulling all his senses and taut muscles into a false sense of peace.

Because no woman ever brought peace to a man's life.

Miraculously, his nervy son's jerky and uncoordinated movements seemed more controlled under her calm guidance. She had a knack with him, a natural ease that he'd never seen in anyone—other than Kate, of course.

All the women he'd introduced to Sam—including the

unnervingly competent Jane—had been unable to get past his son's chilly reserve.

But these two were giggling like conspirators. What was she doing right? he agonised.

Leaning forward, his dark eyes intent on them, he tried to analyse her method. It couldn't be any harder than reading a balance sheet.

'No, there aren't any problems,' she was saying cheerfully. 'I can't keep clutter because I don't have much room here, but then I like to keep my life simple and I've never yearned for a hundred pairs of shoes when I can only wear one pair at a time. It's a choice I've made, Sam. I work to live, instead of living to work.'

Zach's mouth compressed. That would be over his son's head. He wouldn't understand.

'What do you mean?' Sam asked, proving him right.

'You hold the plates, I'll dish up.'

For a moment, he thought scornfully that she had ducked the issue. Then, when the plates were on the table and enticing him with their contents, she spoke again, her face intent and serious.

'I work just enough hours to supply my needs. I want to have leisure time to enjoy my friends and my surroundings.' She smiled. 'That's what matters in the end. Friends and family.'

'You've got children?' asked Sam innocently.

'No. I'm not married. And I don't have parents, either. They're dead. I was brought up in a Children's Home.'

'Oh, that's awful!' Sam declared.

'No, it wasn't!' She laughed. 'I had a whale of a time. More friends than I could wish for. They're my family. And so I make time for them, and the world I live in. If I couldn't sit outside and…say…watch the kingfisher during the day, I'd feel I'd missed something wonderful.'

'Dad works all the time,' Sam declared, clearly having trouble in accepting this alien work ethic.

Catherine's soft, unjudgemental gaze met Zach's. 'I know,' she said gently. 'He's pursuing happiness in his own way.'

Happiness! What did that have to do with work? Angrily he ate a piece of sausage, consuming it at his usual rate—which one of his dates had likened to the speed of sound.

And then he paused. Speared a second piece and chewed more slowly. There had been an explosion of taste in his mouth; subtle herbs, onion—or perhaps leeks—and the best pork he'd tasted this side of a gourmet dinner.

Oblivious to the chatter across the table, he sliced the fried egg which had once been encased in a baby-pink shell. Though its size had nothing to do with babies and everything to do with giant hens. It was certainly the most enormous egg he'd ever seen.

He leaned back when his plate was clean—wiped thoroughly with a hunk of her home-made bread—and waited for the acid discomfort that always attacked him after meals. When it didn't come he realised that he was feeling deeply relaxed. And that—much to his surprise—he was almost smiling as he watched his son enthusiastically accepting the offer of a second egg.

'You're in luck. This one's got a double yolk,' Catherine announced proudly, bringing his son's plate back to the table.

Eagerly Sam tucked in, and he was conscious that both he and Catherine were watching Sam in proud amusement. Their eyes met. They smiled at one another in mutual pleasure. His heart leapt, alarming him.

'Good meal,' he said crisply, as detached as if she were a maître d'.

'The best!' sparkled Sam, putting down his knife and fork with a contented sigh.

She ruffled Sam's hair and it annoyed Zach that his son didn't mind, but grinned up at her adoringly.

'Thank you,' she said, her warmth mainly directed at Sam.

'Tell me which butcher you use,' Zach said, aware that he'd been a little too curt. 'I'd like to put in a regular order for those sausages.'

She smiled. 'They're vegetarian,' she replied, much to his astonishment. 'From the village store.' Eyes twinkling at his dumbstruck expression, she demurely collected up their plates. 'Look…it's such a lovely day. Why don't we sit outside and finish our drinks there?' She pointed through the double cabin doors to the fore deck, which was ablaze with sunshine. 'If we're very still and quiet, we might see the kingfisher.'

'Can we, Dad?' begged Sam, immediately anxious.

Zach tenderly stroked his son's frowning forehead, immeasurably pleased to see the lines disappear as if by magic. He was bonding with his child. Touching him. Reassuring him. So this was how it was done…

'Of course we can,' he said huskily, awash with indulgent love. What did a few more minutes matter if his son was happy? 'I'll wash up later.' He stood aside politely. 'Catherine?' he prompted, when she hung back.

She shook her head, needing a moment to gather herself together. Zach's relationship with Sam tugged at her heartstrings.

'Won't be a second. Just want to check the hot water situation,' she fudged.

Zach climbed up the steps and bowed his head beneath the low cabin doors. He seemed less tense than before, his body moving with fluid power.

She tried to still her clamouring senses. Cooking breakfast had been a simple task. And yet it had seemed to be one of those defining moments in her life.

Encouraging little Sam and with Zach watching approvingly, she had been in seventh heaven. Especially when they had both enjoyed the food so much.

Her feelings had become muddled. They needed sorting out. Why was she so keen to introduce Zach and Sam to her way of life? Why did it matter so much to her? She'd never flung so many facts about homoeopathy at a total stranger before. But she'd wanted Zach to respect what she did.

And even odder, she could understand her motherly feelings towards the little boy, but not why she felt such an irrational yearning to alleviate Zach's stress.

Perhaps it was her healing instincts. People came to her, sick and miserable, and she delighted in seeing them gradually bloom and come alive again.

But, however needy they might be, Sam and Zach were not her patients. They hadn't asked for her help. Her whole life was based on a principle of being unjudgemental. The way Zach chose to live his life was none of her business.

She grinned. She might want to shake him and say that he was destroying himself—and his privileged position as a father—by focusing so much on work, but she really had to keep her nose out!

Her small nose wrinkled instead. So why was she doing her best to prove that he was missing the very essence of life as she lived it?

Because, came the blunt answer, he'd rung all her bells. And she wanted his to ring to the same tune.

'You're a fool!' she breathed to herself.

Then she laughed ruefully and went out into the sunshine to join Zach and Sam on the bench. Zach looked up at her with his intense and mesmeric gaze. The bells pealed joyously and she found herself with a stupid smile on her face.

'It's extraordinarily quiet out here,' he murmured.

'It is. Just the sounds of the river, birdsong and the rustling of the leaves,' she agreed, a little unsteadily.

'Where's this kingfisher, then?' he asked quietly.

Cradling her mug, she nodded towards the bird's favourite perch, a branch that overhung the river.

'It usually sits there.' Her heart pounded and she stilled it with her hand. 'Very quiet, now. Very still.'

The silence enfolded them. The river gurgled and murmured gently. Her hens muttered quietly to themselves in their containers. Rays of sun streamed through the trees, bathing everything in gold. Zach looked transformed, all the lines on his face erased.

She couldn't tear her gaze away. He seemed rapt, those steely eyes soft now as they focused intently on the branch. The strong bone structure of his cheeks and jaw made a little spasm of pleasure knot and twist inside her.

She'd never known anyone with such animal magnetism. Had never felt so unstable and out of control. It was exciting and frightening at the same time. She felt drawn to him—and yet fearful of the maelstrom that might envelop her.

Life would never be simple with Zach. It would be a turbulent roller-coaster of a ride. He had the most intense passions of any man she had ever known. And she didn't think she could handle them.

Slowly his head turned and he met her liquefied gaze, holding it for several long seconds before he frowned and averted his eyes. She flinched. He was annoyed with her.

He'd seen her interest and had been appalled by her presumption.

She felt humiliated. And it was her own fault. Men like Zach weren't for the likes of her to convert from the worship of Mammon. Who was she kidding? He was a lost cause, anyway.

Zach's heart was pumping fit to burst. He cursed himself for dropping his guard. Catherine was leaving. And it was crazy to think that there was anything other than a crude physical attraction between them. She could never understand his needs, his life-style.

Ruefully he acknowledged that if they'd met in any other circumstances they would be flirting now. Making a date.

He would have treated her to candlelit dinners in the best restaurants around. Taken her to a show in London, a première, maybe. A trip to Paris. Bought her a new wardrobe, a car—even an apartment near to his...

Sam's indrawn breath and stiffened body brought Zach back to reality. The kingfisher had appeared. A tiny scrap of iridescence, it peered down into the water with watchful, bright eyes. Suddenly there was a flash of searing blue, as fast as a lightning strike, and the bird had vanished.

Feeling oddly privileged, as though he'd witnessed something momentous, he turned to Sam and quite involuntarily hugged him.

'Did you see it?' he breathed.

'Yes! Dad—! You're grinning!' his son declared in wonder, snuggling deeper into his father's arms.

'Well, it was special. Wasn't it?' he muttered gruffly.

'Your frown's gone,' said Sam happily. Zach felt it reappear and a small finger came up to rub it away. 'Don't, Dad. You look scary when you do that.'

A jerk of pain made his chest ache. 'I'll try not to,' he said softly. He made a face. 'I just have a lot to think about. By the end of the day I'll have a monumental back-up of calls on my mobile.'

He could have kicked himself. Sam had flinched and moved away. How stupid could he be? It had just been a comment but it must have sounded as if he was fretting about work. Two days ago he would have let that remark lie. Today he felt bold enough to risk rejection.

'Still, who cares?' he said lightly, grabbing Sam's limp hand. 'I'd rather be here, with you.'

'Would you, Dad?'

Tearful pale eyes searched his and Zach put all his heart and soul into his gaze.

'Course I would,' he said gruffly. 'And we'll have a day to remember. But first, I promised to wash up. Why don't you and Catherine have that tour while I get acquainted with the sink?' he added with a smile.

'Good idea,' Catherine agreed with a peculiar heartiness. 'Then I must get that engine going and be off—or you'll never see the back of me.'

He registered Sam's look of horror, the way he clutched at Catherine's skirt and lifted his dismayed face to hers.

'You're not leaving?' Sam cried in protest.

Gently her hand caressed the small, pale face. 'I must. I can't stay—'

'Why not? Why can't she, Dad?'

He floundered, unwilling to condemn himself in his son's eyes.

'Because…well, it's like this…'

Catherine generously saved him. 'I need a proper site. Somewhere else to tie up—'

'But this is nice, isn't it?'

'Ye-es, Sam—' she agreed awkwardly.

'Then you can stay here! Can't she, Dad?' Sam cried.

'We can't keep Catherine if she needs to leave,' he muttered.

'But she doesn't *want* to go. You must be able to see that. Her eyes went all watery. And I don't want her to go, either,' Sam said grumpily. 'Tell him!' he insisted, tugging Catherine's skirt. 'Tell him you want to stay!'

Zach met the intense blaze of his son's steel grey eyes with a sober gaze. On this he would be judged. His relationship with his son hung by a thread.

It was a case of being a hero in Sam's eyes, or playing safe. Because, if Catherine stayed, he knew he'd find it hard to keep away from her. There was something about her that pulled him closer, despite all his efforts not to be attracted.

That went against all logic. He had been weak once and his world had fallen apart. It had taken a long time to build it up again.

Nothing and no one would hurt him again. He'd see to that. Barriers were his speciality. He'd had plenty of practice in shutting women out of his life...

A pair of hot little hands settled on his knees. Sam was close to tears and on impulse Zach drew his son close in a comforting hug.

'You can't expect people to stay around just because you want them to,' he said with infinite tenderness. The scrawniness of his child jerked at his heart. He would give him the world if it would make him happy. That was more important than stray sexual urges he might feel for unsuitable females. 'However...'

His eyes met Catherine's in a query. Trying not to be affected by her charm, he said in a deliberately detached tone, 'If she doesn't mind staying here for a little while then that's fine by me. Although she will need to find somewhere else. A proper, permanent site.' He paused and calculated. Four weekends with Sam should do it. By then the two of them would be close. 'Could you manage… say…a month?'

There was a tense silence while he and Sam waited for her response. He felt the erratic fluttering of his son's heart against his chest and tried to calm him by caressing the dark head pressed hard into his shoulder.

Watching them, Catherine gave a sudden smile of such radiance that he had to swallow the lump that came into his throat.

'That sounds fine. I would like to take you up on that offer,' she said softly and he felt as if he were bathed in light. 'Thank you very much.'

He was nearly throttled by a pair of wiry arms that wrapped around his neck.

'Dad, oh, Dad! We can come and see Catherine every day when I visit!'

Suddenly released, he saw Catherine suffer the same fate. She had caught Sam in her arms and lifted him up and he was hugging her as if she'd filled his pockets with gold.

'We can do that, can't we? We'll be very good and not get in your way or—'

'You are more than welcome to visit me,' she said lovingly, her eyes glistening. 'You too, Zach,' she added with equal warmth. 'Any time.'

His head went into a spin and he tried to make it settle so he could make sense of what had happened. She was too accommodating. Too eager. But then, he argued, she had everything to win and nothing to lose.

Somehow she'd manoeuvred the situation so that he'd been obliged to let her moor her darn boat to his island. Before he knew it, she'd have half the countryside beating a path to her door and the banks would be strung with the mooring ropes of every stray narrow boat in England.

'I'm doing this for my son,' he said coolly, so that she was in no doubt.

'And he's thrilled,' she acknowledged. 'You've made him very happy.'

Zach grunted. In a world of his own, Sam was dreamily trailing his fingers in the water, leaning perilously over the side.

'And you,' he drawled. 'You've got what you want.'

She seemed to flinch. 'Is that how you see it?' she asked, all round-eyed and innocent.

'That's how it is,' he replied sardonically.

Her chin lifted and her expression became chilly.

'I'll show Sam around,' she muttered. He felt almost disappointed that she hadn't continued to protest her innocence. Presumably she knew she hadn't a leg to stand on. She rose, every inch the aggrieved Ice Queen. 'The washing up liquid is under the sink,' she added, collecting Sam and leading him into the cabin.

At least she knew where she stood, he thought in satisfaction, following them after a decent interval. She knew he was on to her wheedling ways.

And there would be no more lingering looks on his part. She was a means to an end. His son's emotional happiness.

Still smarting from Zach's insulting suggestion that she'd used Sam for her own ends, she decided to annoy him by spending ages showing the little boy around.

He tried every cupboard door, sat in her easy chair and the comfortable bench, then when she'd converted the bench into the bed he even tried that. The heavy iron door to the stove was heaved open and the neatly laid wood and coal inside duly admired.

Deliberately, Zach went out to the fore deck when he'd finished the chores. Catherine's murmuring voice was beginning to slide under his defences. It had a wonderful soothing quality—probably part of her professional manner—and it annoyed him that he kept wanting to be part of her tour.

So, to prove his inner strength and indifference to female charms, he excluded himself from it completely.

Leaning back on the comfortable bench, he closed his eyes and let the sun warm his lids. Already he was beginning to identify the sounds around him. The ripple of water as a duck scurried by. The hens cracking their beaks quietly. A soft plop as an unidentifiable fish surfaced and grabbed at an unsuspecting insect admiring its reflection in the river.

He opened his eyes at an odd trilling sound. Two little brown birds were processing along the river, doing that up-ending thing that ducks did, so that just their tails were visible as they hunted beneath the surface for…whatever ducks ate. He felt a little put out by his lack of knowledge and hoped Sam didn't expect him to be an expert on the countryside.

'Aren't they smashing?'

He found that he was already smiling broadly when he turned to Sam, who was eyeing the ducks with fascination.

'Cute,' he agreed.

'Dabchicks,' Sam said, proud of his new knowledge.

'Ah.' He stood up, excited about the prospect of having the whole day with his son. 'Come on, Sam. We have things to do. You need to find a suitable place on the island to build a camp. And then we must plan a tree house…'

'Wow!' His son's slight frame cannoned into his, accompanied by a loud whoop.

Yes, he thought, meeting Catherine's heart-jerkingly tender eyes. He owed her. He couldn't deny that.

'Thank you,' he mouthed over Sam's head while his son tried to squeeze the life out of him.

Her chocolate drop eyes melted and her smile oozed silkily into his body, destroying its barriers. Time to get away.

'Say goodbye for now,' he instructed Sam. 'There's a lot to do before you go home.'

Catherine hugged the little boy briefly and immediately hurried back through the boat. For a moment she paused to do a bit of deep breathing till her hands stopped shaking in such a stupid way.

There was no doubt about it. Her heart was deeply touched by Zach's joyous smile at his son's pleasure. He might be driven and ambitious, but he did care passionately about his child. And for that she could forgive him much.

Perhaps even like him.

She felt elated and knew why. It wasn't because she could enjoy the island for another month and could therefore repaint the sides as she'd planned, but because she'd almost certainly see Zach during that time. He intrigued her more than anyone she'd ever known. There was a loving heart concealed beneath that granite exterior, of that she was sure.

Perhaps Edith had known that. Catherine caught her breath. The old lady had been very astute. It was quite possible that she'd given Zach the island because she knew it could change his life for the better.

She remembered something Edith had said, and which had puzzled her at the time—'You do trust me to do the best for the island, don't you? Whatever happens, have faith in me. I think you'll find I've made a sound judgement.'

Catherine's excitement increased. Edith had met Zach several times, presumably, and had judged that Zach would be a worthy owner of her beloved island.

There must be a very special person lurking under Zach's stern exterior. She smiled dreamily, thinking that it would be a fascinating process, seeing that person emerge.

Four weeks. That was all she had. She leant back against the ticket drawer, half-scared to trust her instincts. Because all along they had been trying to tell her that this man was special and that somewhere in that scowling high-flier there was a heart so big and a personality so dazzling that no other man would ever match him.

The swell of happiness that surged through her was frightening. She could be wrong. Edith could be mistaken. But…life was for living. She had to trust her intuition. Even though she felt she was poised to jump off a cliff into an abyss.

CHAPTER EIGHT

TEMPTED though she was to 'accidentally' bump into Zach and Sam that day, she controlled her longing and left them firmly alone. They needed to be together, father and son.

She thought fondly of the pleasure Zach would have, and that a little bit of his carefully guarded heart would be melted by the end of the day.

In a fever of activity she fixed the engine, made some bread and put it to rise, then energetically sanded down the side door panels which bore the name of the boat and its fleet number. Feeling pleased with the start she'd made, she started up the engine again and took a trial trip down the river.

'Catherine! Look at us!' squealed a familiar voice as she approached the little copse on the island.

'Hello, Sam! Zach!' She waved madly, her eyes misting over to see Zach with his arm proudly around his son's shoulders.

'We're making a camp! Come and see!'

She hesitated. Urged on by Sam, Zach beckoned. And she couldn't refuse, could she? Throwing the boat into reverse to stop it, she eased the tiller over and swung close to the bank.

As if born to boat life Zach leapt on board, flinging a rope to Sam, then scrambled back to tie it to a tree. Catherine finished sliding the narrow boat alongshore and fastened the stern rope as well.

'Come on, come *on*!' Sam cried impatiently, dragging her along.

'He's terribly excited,' she murmured to Zach, her eyes shining with pleasure.

'Delirious,' came the curt reply.

She smiled to herself. Zach was a master of caution. And yet the glow in his face betrayed the fact that he was thrilled too.

'You are both absolutely filthy!' she pointed out with a giggle.

'I know.'

With a near smile, he glanced down at the muddied jeans, the shirt smeared with lichen stains where he'd clearly carried branches for the camp.

'There it is!'

'Oh, Sam!' she cried, clasping her hands in awe. 'It's far grander than I ever imagined!'

'Dad's idea. Look. There's a door that opens and this'll be a window when we're finished—'

The little boy chattered on, describing everything in detail. She was amazed. Far from being a heap of wood leaning precariously to form a kind of cave, this 'den' had a proper roof and the sides had been fixed with nails.

Her heart began to thud. It wasn't a temporary structure, to amuse his son for a few weekends. This was permanent.

'You've built this so well!' she marvelled, opening and closing the door and sticking her fingers through the letterbox.

Zach shrugged and tried to look modest. 'My father could turn his hand to anything. I used to fetch and carry for him when he did DIY till I went away to school.'

A small hand dragged her inside. 'Chairs! And look, a proper table! And Dad's promised to build more furniture from scraps of wood this week. Now we're going to make a fire then we'll get potatoes to bake in it for high tea! Isn't it brill?'

'Brill,' she agreed warmly. 'You really are having a fabulous day, aren't you, Sam?'

'The best! Shall I get a potato for you?'

'Catherine's on her way somewhere,' Zach said quickly and with an unmistakable veto in his warning eyes. 'Glad you fixed the engine,' he added with studied politeness.

Disappointed though she was, she took the hint. This was Zach's day to be a father. She couldn't begrudge him that.

'Yes. So am I glad! Well, Robinson Crusoes, I am off. Thank you for showing me your camp. I think it's wonderful.'

At the end of the day Zach and Sam cleaned themselves up in the comfortable kitchen, thankful for the warmth of the stove. Over the last half hour the air had turned chilly and a faint dampness had crept like a moving veil over the river.

'I'm so tired!' sighed Sam blissfully, leaning against his father.

Overcome with love, he hugged his son and held him for a golden moment.

'Me too. Good, though, wasn't it? Now,' he sighed reluctantly, 'we must get your coat on. Your mother will be arriving any minute. We'll meet her on the other side of the river, shall we?' He bent his head and smelled the mixture of soap and child that so delighted him. 'You'll have loads to tell her.'

His heart turned over at the glow in Sam's eyes and the enormous grin that lit the pale face. Except it wasn't pale now, but pink and healthy. Zach wondered if a city life was entirely suitable for a child. And he began to think that he might keep Tresanton Island for a permanent weekend bolt hole.

With mist wreathing about his ankles a short time later he waved goodbye to Sam, knowing that this had been a turning point in their relationship.

A lump came into his throat and he stood by the bridge, waving as frantically as his son until the car was out of sight.

'Thank you, Edith,' he muttered under his breath, understanding at last why she'd gifted the island to him. In doing so, she had given him his son back. There was no value you could put on something like that.

Ignoring his furiously vibrating phone—as he'd done so all day—he hurried back to the warm and welcoming house. He needed just a little more time to himself before he launched into the financial world again. And then he'd work through the night to catch up with the backlog. He pulled a sweater over his shirt and poured himself a glass of wine.

He was still sitting at the kitchen table, his mind drifting, when he heard a rapping on the back door. Looking up, he recognised the small, slender form of Catherine.

Steady, he warned himself as his breath shortened. Keep the barrier up. Stay safe, unhurt, focused.

'Yes?' he asked curtly when he'd opened the door a crack.

'Could I see you for a minute?' she asked meekly.

He found a frown, despite the sweetness of her face. 'I'm busy.'

'It won't take long.' She wrapped her arms around herself, a hessian bag swinging weightily from one hand. 'Please?'

Catherine gave an involuntary shiver and he noticed then that she'd changed into a honey-coloured skirt of some soft material that brushed the tops of her shoes. Like the matching jersey shirt she wore, it was clearly not warm enough for the fresh evening.

Although she was hugging herself he could see that she wasn't wearing a bra. The cold air had hardened her nipples so that they were pushing against the soft fabric.

Trying not to weaken like his treacherously succumbing body he opened the door wider but made no move to ask her in.

'Well?'

He was quite pleased with that 'well?' He'd put all his effort into sounding irritated, despite the fact that his emotions were urging him to invite her in for a drink—two, three, a cosy chat…perhaps more…

It worried him that his eyes might have softened, because she was smiling that wall-breaking smile. He pushed out a scowl to counteract it.

'Zach, I realise this is perhaps inconvenient,' she said softly, 'but I am absolutely freezing. I hadn't realised it was so chilly out. Could I just step inside before I catch pneumonia and die a terrible and lingering death on your doorstep?'

She wanted something. Another favour. He let his eyes flicker briefly with cynicism.

'If you must.'

Demurely she stepped over the threshold though he still barred her way, his folded arms helping him to maintain his aloofness to her tiny, trembling form which cried out for the protection of his arms and the warmth of his body.

'Could I snuggle up to the Aga?' she pleaded, her teeth chattering. 'Early May can be so treacherous where weather's concerned. Fickle.' She arched an eyebrow at him. 'Doesn't seem to know what it wants to do. Warm one moment, cold the next.'

Was that a reference to him? He wouldn't put it past her. She was clever, he knew that.

With a carefully resigned sigh to show his irritation, he stepped aside. She sank to her knees in front of the oven, her skirts pooling about her like liquid honey as she rubbed her hands gratefully over one of the shiny red doors.

Her waist was tiny. He could see her spine just outlined through the stretchy material of her shirt. Her hands were very elegant, her arms graceful in every movement. The river ripple of her hair seemed designed to be stroked and he felt an overwhelming urge to crouch down beside her, enfold her in his arms and bury his face in its perfumed tresses. Then to taste the glide of her neck, her jawline and…

He looked longingly at her mouth, contemplating the feel of it. She was smiling to herself, as though her mind was full of memories.

'You know, Edith and I used to do this in the winter,' she mused softly, 'after we'd been—'

'What do you want?' he broke in abruptly.

Catherine felt as if he'd slapped her face. Courtesy would be nice, she thought, upset by his response. A tiny hint of a social grace.

'I was only reminiscing,' she said, her voice shaky.

'I told you. I'm busy.'

Subdued by his abruptness, by his lack of interest in Edith—or her—she rose to her feet and reached mechanically into her hessian bag.

'Right. Sorry. I brought you some eggs.' Diving into the depths of the bag, she pulled out the box. 'And bread. It's still warm,' she said flatly.

To her relief, his mouth did move in the direction of a smile, even if it stopped long before one was properly formed. He sniffed at the bread and broke off a piece of crust, chewing it with skilfully concealed pleasure. But his eyes were appreciative and she relaxed a little. He was all bark and no bite, she decided, her hopes rising.

'Thanks. Why?' he shot out.

Catherine's eyes widened and she blinked. 'Why what?'

'Why are you giving me this?'

Wryly she noticed he didn't return her gifts. 'It's a neighbourly thing to do,' she answered, working overtime to remain calm and even-tempered. 'A friendly gesture.'

'And what do you want in return?'

Her mouth compressed as she composed something cutting in reply. And then she grinned. He was right. She was intent on bribery!

'Guilty,' she admitted with a laugh and leaned back against the stove. 'I hadn't seen it like that. Around here we always take little gifts—'

'What,' he interrupted coldly, 'do you want?'

'To clear up a small point—'

'Which is? And how small?' he growled, pulling off another chunk of bread.

'You've very kindly let me stay for a month,' she began.

'Purely because you and your boat amuse Sam,' he explained hurriedly.

'I know,' she agreed, her face soft as she recalled the little boy's enchanting eagerness. 'He's a lovely kiddie. You've had a good day, I imagine. How were the potatoes?'

Zach visibly relaxed. 'Best we've ever tasted.' He laughed at a private joke and she held her breath, dazzled by his happiness. 'They were black on the outside and uncooked on the inside but we ate every scrap!'

She laughed too. 'I'm glad it was a success,' she said in a low tone.

'It was.' His curtness had returned. 'Thank you for the idea.'

If only he would drop his role as the driven financier and stick with being a loving father! She hated one. Liked the other. Very much.

'*You* carried the idea out—and in a spectacular fashion,' she told him quietly.

'I enjoyed it too,' he said to himself, as though that surprised him.

She sighed with pleasure. 'That's wonderful.' A tremor shook the warm sincerity in her voice.

Slowly raising his head, he looked at her and a silence fell as their gazes meshed and held. But it was a tense hush, the air electric between them.

'So, Catherine. What do you want of me?' he asked throatily.

Catherine fought to remember, her startled eyes huge as she weakened beneath his sultry scrutiny. I want it all, she thought, with sudden honesty. Everything he has to offer.

'I—I…' It came to her. Somehow she dragged her brain out of reverse and got down to business. 'It's about the path from the bridge.' She waited for an encouraging response but didn't get one so she continued. 'The fact is that I don't know if my patients can still use it and come to see me while I'm here. You didn't say. I'd be grateful if they could, then I can keep my appointments going for this month and I'll have time to make other arrangements for when I leave.'

He seemed to be weighing up his answer and trying to decide whether to grant her plea or deny it. Tense and nervous, she watched four powerful inhalations of his breath and four exhalations before he was ready to reply.

'No.'

She slumped, shocked by the depth of her disappointment. Stark-eyed, she stared at him, hoping to see a sign that he might relent. Cold and hard, his flint eyes stared back unflinchingly.

'I could pay you some rent—' she offered.

'No.'

And that, as far as he was concerned, seemed to be his final decision.

'You don't waste words, do you?' she muttered crossly.

'Life's too short.'

'It's for living!' she cried passionately and yes, there, she caught a brief flash of a reaction, a passionate longing which was just as quickly brought under control.

'I have calls to make.'

'I'm sure you have.' She sighed.

Extraordinarily depressed, she turned to go. All day, she realised gloomily, she'd harboured stupid, irrational little fantasies in the back of her mind. And they had all included Zach telling her she could stay after all. And she'd predicted that he'd mellow under the influence of the island and they'd fall madly in love and...

Oh, what was the use? She'd made a terrible mistake. He wasn't special at all. Edith had been wrong.

Worse than that, her whole livelihood was now threatened.

'I'll see you out,' he muttered, striding stiffly to the door and holding it open.

It looked bleak outside. She shrank into herself. 'Goodbye,' she mumbled, glum-faced. 'I might have known it would come to this. If I can't work, then I might as well leave the island tomorrow. I can't live on air.' And she headed for the door, her heart in her boots.

'*No!*'

With that fierce rocket of a word Zach shot out a hand and stopped her in mid-stride. Startled, she looked back at him, surprised to see an expression of panic in his eyes.

'No,' he said, more quietly but with tight emphasis.

She found her other arm imprisoned by his firm grip and then she had been swung around to face him. It was beneath her dignity to resist. Instead, she stood there scornfully meeting his fiery eyes.

His plans were going awry and he didn't like that. He thought she'd be a pushover and she'd do as he wanted, did he? That an order from him would bully her into abject submission?

Her face set in mutinous lines. She wasn't one of his minions, to be issued instructions on how, when and where to do his bidding! No one had ever pushed her around and they weren't going to start now. Least of all this selfish, egocentric, arrogant City slicker who had his brain full of figures and a heart that beat eagerly to the tune of clinking coins.

'I have to go, you must see that! You leave me no choice!' she bit out.

'I don't want you to,' he said with a scowl.

'I bet. My boat and my chickens interest Sam too much, don't they?' she snapped waspishly.

A strange bitterness seemed to be eating into her heart. Yet she'd known—had even welcomed—the fact that Zach and Sam had needed help. Why should she now feel so hurt when Zach wanted to keep her as a source of amusement for his son?

'I've already said that. You are the equivalent of the local theme park to him, yes,' he growled.

Her eyes were scathing. 'Now I'm a minor tourist attraction, am I?'

At least he had the grace to look slightly abashed. 'You said you would stay. I assumed it was a promise that would be kept.' Craftily, he added, 'Are you in the habit of disappointing children?'

Catherine glared. They seemed to be closer suddenly, his warmth invading her space and making her flounder just when it was important for her to keep her wits about her. She gritted her teeth.

'Naturally I would have left a letter explaining to him why I had to leave after all,' she muttered. 'He'd understand that I have to work. And that *your* refusal was preventing me,' she added defiantly. 'And don't offer me money to tide me over. I won't accept it. Now let me go. I have to prepare the boat. *Again.*'

'Don't do this!' he blurted out hoarsely.

His eyes burned feverishly into hers. She reeled from his passion for his son. And felt moved by it, too. But he was using her for his own ends and she wouldn't stand for that. There had to be an equal arrangement between them...

An idea occurred to her. She lifted her head and looked him directly in the eyes. For a moment she faltered, because they were dark and pained and she felt compassion for him. His great love for his son touched her deeply. He'd do anything for Sam. Perhaps even change his mind.

'You want me to stay,' she said slowly, marshalling her thoughts.

His eyes glowed as if he had detected her surrender.

'Yes!' he muttered with low passion.

She swallowed, shaken by the intensity of his feelings.

'I want to stay, too—though for an entirely different reason.'

She wished she could sound crisp and businesslike and not as husky as a sixty a day smoker. Whatever was the matter with her throat?

'That's…' He checked himself, the flashing smile and brilliant light in his eyes dimming considerably as his self-control overcame any foolish display of pleasure. 'That's good—'

'I haven't finished,' she interrupted icily and his face turned to stone. 'I *will* stay and be a theme park attraction whenever your son comes here…' She paused, disconcerted by the leap of joy in his expression. How he loved his child! There was good in him then…

'I sense there's a ''but'' or an ''if'' coming,' he said drily.

The grip on her arms became less confining. Unfortunately, he was so engrossed in the possibility of getting his own way that he was absently rubbing his thumbs backwards and forwards across her tingling flesh.

Catherine tried desperately to steady her racing pulses. 'You're right. It is an ''if''. Let's make a deal. You must be used to those. I will stay—providing you give me temporary use of the bridge path so that I can continue my treatments. You must understand, Zach. There must be something in this for me. Otherwise I'm off.'

He looked down at her, reluctant to grant any favours. But she knew that his love for Sam would win the day.

'Very clever.'

'I thought so,' she acknowledged.

She'd intended to sound calm and detached. To her ears, her husky voice had been decidedly shaky.

But there was a glint of humour in his eyes and a faint lift to his suddenly carnal mouth.

'Done!' he said decisively.

She was released so abruptly that she staggered back a

little. And only then did she realise that she'd been holding her breath and every muscle she possessed had been squeezed tightly in tension.

Clutching at a handy chair back to help support her shaky legs, she watched Zach stride across the kitchen to the bottle of wine on the counter top, his entire body bursting with barely controlled delight.

He found a glass and brought it over with the wine. His mood seemed strange. A mixture of taut exhilaration and annoyance. She supposed that made sense. He'd be pleased to have his theme park attraction and annoyed that he'd had to make a concession!

The glass was thrust at her without charm, his burning eyes piercing hers in a stare so powerful that her knees began to wobble.

'You know I have no choice,' he said abruptly. 'I must agree to your bargain.' Apparently hot, he stripped off his jumper and flung it to one side. Then he sipped his wine, never once taking his eyes from her. 'But let's get this clear. It is just for a month.'

'Clear.'

'No longer.'

'Agreed.'

She could be as curt as he. But in her case it was because her throat was closing up. Zach towered over her, dominating the room, overwhelming her entire body with his extraordinary presence.

'No riotous parties.'

'No.'

Had he come a step closer? It seemed the gap between them had filled with a thick and electrifying heat. Catherine clung frantically to her glass, bending her head and sipping the wine in the hope that it would take centre stage, instead of Zach.

'Nobody is to wander about the island unless it's you—and then only with my permission.'

'Right.'

Her ears were playing her up. He had sounded as husky as she. Desperate to force herself away, she flashed him a quick glance. And found herself paralysed and unable to move. Her lips quivered and parted.

'Keep…out of…my hair,' he muttered. And his hands lifted slowly, coming to rest on her trembling shoulders.

'Yes,' she whispered.

Her face had lifted to his. The closeness of his mouth made her head whirl.

'Next weekend. As part of your duties…'

There was a long pause and she waited, her nerves stretched to their limits.

'Uh huh?' she prompted. And when he still didn't answer, she croaked out, 'Duties?'

'Oh. Yes, I thought…maybe a boat…trip.'

She closed her eyes and nodded dumbly, knowing that nothing coherent could ever emerge from her throat. And then she felt something brush her lips. Something warm. Soft yet firm.

Her skin tingled. She dare not open her eyes. Dare not move, but stood there, willing, hoping, and wantonly available.

Because every fibre of her being was crying out for Zach to touch her, hold her, and make passionate love to her—even though she knew she'd be nothing more to him than a passing fancy.

And that afterwards she'd regret every moment.

CHAPTER NINE

SHE was willing. They were adults, Zach argued, his conscience still making a hash of fighting his physical urges. His brain seemed to be in tangles and knots and he couldn't think straight. But he had to.

He clenched his jaw and did his best. This had to be stopped. Now. And yet…why deny himself?

Catherine wasn't conventional. She probably believed in free love—and he wanted her more than he'd ever wanted any woman in the whole of his life.

How he'd stopped himself from ripping all her clothes off, he didn't know. Except that he wanted this to be slow and exploratory and to be the best lover she'd ever known…

'This is a purely business arrangement,' he said, intending to sound stern but he was too close to that beautiful mouth for anything but a soft murmur to emerge.

'Mm-hmm,' she agreed.

The flutter of her lashes and her sigh was his downfall. How could he resist? Flesh and blood met in a sudden fiery embrace. Slow and languid it was not. Closer to torrid.

His mouth and hers became irretrievably joined and he groaned at the sweet taste of her, the softness of her willowy body, the tantalising scent that rose from her skin and hair.

'Nothing permanent,' he croaked thickly.

'Nnnn,' she breathed into his mouth.

And her hands wound around his neck, drawing his

head down more firmly, demanding the same kind of fierce passion that boiled in his veins.

We are matched, he thought dizzily. She seemed to fit his embrace and his body as if she'd been made for him. There was nothing clumsy about their exploration of one another's mouths. Just a perfect knowing, as if they'd been synchronised and rehearsed by a choreographer, with each passionate and near-desperate kiss sliding smoothly into the next.

His hand stole up her thigh. Touched silken skin, as hot as his fingers. She flung her head back and he kissed her throat with gentle reverence. Without another word, he took her hand and led her upstairs.

'Zach,' she whispered uncertainly, seeming to realise suddenly that they were in his bedroom.

But he gathered her to him and coaxed her trembling mouth apart, whispering to her.

'You are so beautiful. Feel so good. Taste...' he emerged breathless and dizzy from a long, deep kiss '...like nothing else on earth. I could kiss you for hours. Hold you in my arms and just enjoy the way our bodies melt together.'

In the back of his mind he was startled by himself. He'd never spoken like that before. Never felt so lyrical about sex. He felt alarmed. It was sweeping him along like a river in full spate and he had no control any more.

Just when he was on the brink of drawing away she looked deep into his eyes with such a melting joy that he shook. Her fingers slipped between the buttons of his shirt and he impatiently ripped it open, frantic to feel her palms on his chest, the softness of her cheek against his pounding heart.

And as if reading his mind, this is what she did. First, a wandering exploration of his torso, tracing the contours.

Then her mouth following the path her fingers had taken. And finally she listened to his heart while he cradled her head with one hand and inhaled the lemony scent of her shampoo.

He stood her back a little, mesmerised by her shining eyes and sifting his fingers through her glossy waves where they hung close to the slender fragility of her neck.

'Catherine,' he murmured, his head swimming.

Her finger touched his lips. He kissed it, then enclosed her mouth with his, lifting her in his arms at the same time. She was as light as a feather and when he laid her gently on the bed he felt suddenly unsure, even though they were both collaborating in undressing her.

He drew in his breath as her soft shirt fell open to reveal small, high and perfect breasts. Helpless to resist, he bent his head with a groan and nurtured each one with his mouth and tongue and fingers, thrilling when they leapt with touching eagerness to his caresses.

She had shed her skirt and his urging body could feel the heat of her, writhing against him. But she was so fragile! Her bones felt as if they'd snap too easily. He caught her small face in his and willed her to open her eyes.

'Catherine! Catherine!' he said huskily, and two drowsy, sultry dark eyes were suddenly melting his loins. He held back. With difficulty. 'I don't want to hurt you,' he whispered.

'You won't,' she breathed and, closing her eyes again in bliss, she touched him.

Inch by inch he explored and so did she. The sweet pain of waiting made him ache with longing. She began to moan, to demand, to beg him with an intensity that shook him to the very core.

Sensitively, slowly, he slid within her, his lungs emptying as he uttered a ragged groan of relief at the final promise. On the edge of losing control, he managed to coax and caress her until he knew it was the right time to let go.

And then sheer instinct took over, his body moving with hers in a harmony he could never have imagined. And evoking such erotic sensations that he heard himself in the dim distance saying extraordinary things; words of wonder, disbelief and infinite tenderness.

It was someone else who had taken him over. Not him.

Together they clung and gasped and climbed higher and higher until every sense erupted in pleasure.

Together they lay, sweat-slicked and panting, their exhausted and sated bodies slowly subsiding into a deep contentment.

And he began to think. To fear what he had done, and how he had felt. This had been something extraordinary and beyond his understanding. Although he'd tried not to let it happen, there had seemed to be an inevitability about it. And, quite reasonably, he had imagined that since she had seemed willing she was probably experienced and therefore the sex would be good—especially as he seemed to be so hungry.

Yet it had been more than a roll in the hay. He had discovered a sense of caring. She had found a different side to him, a better person. Amazingly, for a short time he had felt a giant among men and that had been a sensation he wanted to cling to.

More profoundly, he felt…connected to her. His body chilled.

'Penny,' she murmured in an appealing little slur that made his heart lurch unnervingly.

'Mmm?' He pretended to look puzzled, giving himself time to think of a suitable response.

'Penny. For your thoughts.'

He turned his head and wished he didn't drown in her chocolate drop eyes.

'Are you cold?' he asked politely.

She smiled. Everything in her face lit up and he felt his solar plexus contract.

'I won't be in a second,' she purred.

When she snuggled up to him, her head tucked beneath his chin, he released a taut breath and almost surrendered to the needs of his emotions. Because he wanted to clutch her to his heart and whisper sweet nothings in her ear. He wanted them to cuddle all night. Maybe sex, but not essentially. Just Catherine and him. Together in his bed.

Him; the giant among men. Catherine; the creator of giants.

She sighed. Then eased herself away. 'I have to go,' she said, her hair swinging forward like a concealing curtain.

Inexplicably insulted that she didn't share his longings, he pushed back the gleaming waves and frowned at her siren face.

'Fine,' he said, trying to sound as if he didn't care.

She giggled, sliding sensuously up his body and pressing her fingers between his brows to smooth out the dark anger there.

'Don't do that!' she crooned. 'I must check the chickens, Zach.'

'Chickens.'

'Yes!' Her smile faded and she looked unsure of herself. Which softened his heart completely. 'Do I...say goodnight, or...do we have other things to...discuss?' she asked in a small voice.

He couldn't resist the thought of a whole night with her in his arms. It wouldn't hurt. He'd probably gone over the top about his emotions because it had been so long since he'd made love to a woman. And she had less guile than most.

'Quite a lot to…er…discuss, you wanton woman,' he said with a grin, doing his best to turn this into a sexual adventure and nothing more. 'Why don't you bring your toothbrush in case it's too late for you to get a cab home?'

Her laughter delighted him. Her kiss increased that delight.

'I'll see you soon,' she whispered into his mouth.

'Very soon,' he breathed back. 'Take a shower before you go, if you like.'

'No. I ought to dash. Perhaps…later.'

He watched her slipping on her clothes, marvelling at the way her limbs moved with such fluidity.

'Borrow one of my jackets from the hall,' he called as she headed for the door. 'It'll be even colder now.'

Turning, she beamed at him, lighting up his entire body with her radiance.

'That's very thoughtful of you. What a sweet man you are,' she murmured. 'Thank you.' And with a little flutter of her hand she left.

When she sleepily stirred the next morning she reached out for Zach in vain. Disappointed by his absence and wishing they could just lie together and chat, she pulled his pillow to her and held it close, breathing in the smell of him.

A small movement startled her. Jerking her head around, she saw him standing fully dressed by the window, his face unreadable.

'Hello,' she said softly, blushing that he'd been watching her.

'I've got work to do,' he muttered, back to his old, repressed self again.

'Me too! I have chickens to feed,' she cried merrily.

She wouldn't entrap him. She'd rely on his tender inner nature to surface again. As if she slept with virtual strangers every day and thought nothing of it, she leapt from the bed and unselfconsciously stood naked in the middle of the room.

'OK if I shower again?' she asked.

Zach seemed about to say something. His eyes had certainly blazed with hunger.

'Sure. I've had my breakfast. Help yourself. I need to call New York.'

She gave him a long look. 'Isn't it the middle of the night, there?' she enquired mildly.

His eyes flickered. 'I meant Tokyo.'

Catherine nodded, disregarding the excuse. She judged that he was scared of what had happened between them. And rightly so. It had been amazing: the sex, the sweetness he'd shown to her and the astonishing glimpses of the wonderful man beneath the image he showed to the world.

She wanted that man to emerge into the light and never hide again.

'I might see you around,' she flung casually, on her way to the en suite bathroom.

'Possibly.'

She shut the door behind her and leaned against it till her heart ceased thumping inside her rib cage. Zach couldn't be hurried. If she wanted him to throw himself heart and soul into their relationship then she must be patient. A slow smile spread over her happy face. He was more than worth the wait.

Every second that morning she hoped to see him but

presumably he'd turned into a walking automaton again and was wasting satellite time with those hedge fund thingies.

The rain was unrelenting and had turned the paths into a quagmire. Luckily her patients were amiable and hadn't protested when she'd suggested they bring their wellington boots.

Even Lady Christabel cheerfully pounded through the morass and arrived on time for her appointment, all smiles and dripping waterproofs.

'Don't mind at all,' she insisted, when Catherine apologised for the state of the path. 'You've brought me back to health. A year ago, I would have had hysterics. Today I can accept minor irritations like torrential rain and mud with a big grin and an umbrella.'

Catherine laughed and for the first time that morning she truly relaxed, chatting contentedly to Lady Christabel as she worked on her lymph glands. She thought that she, too could accept setbacks and put her trust in her intuitive feelings.

In Zach's arms the previous night she had been absolutely sure that they were meant for one another. She'd felt unbelievably cherished and special. And, try as he might, he hadn't been able to hide how moved he'd been by the whole experience.

She bade a fond farewell to Lady Christabel, slid away the treatment bed and quickly filled in the necessary notes, closing the huge book with a satisfied thump because she had seen all of her patients for that day.

She slipped off her shoes and padded around in her socks. Tea and scones were in the offing and then—

She jumped at a sharp rap on the door, her heart in her mouth.

'Please let it be Zach!' she whispered under her breath and adjusted her joyous smile to something less obvious.

'Hello! Quick, you'd better come in!' she said in a friendly-but-not-desperate way.

Shedding water all over the cabin floor, he stared at her as though he didn't really know why he'd come. She smiled affectionately at his frown.

'Here,' she said, taking over and feeling she was clucking like one of her hens. 'You're soaking. Don't you possess a hat or an umbrella?'

He pursed his lips in thought and let her unbutton his raincoat.

'Somewhere,' he said vaguely.

'Shoes off. And next time you're in town, buy some boots, for heaven's sake!' she scolded. 'Now your socks.'

She stuffed newspaper in the sodden shoes and put them near the boiler. The socks were draped over the rack and his raincoat found the hook she'd placed in the shower for just that purpose.

'Tea and scones. They're almost done.'

'Catherine—' he croaked.

'Warm yourself first. Talk later,' she soothed, seeing he looked harrowed.

And she put on some gentle background music after bullying Zach into her most comfortable armchair. It was lovely fussing over him, though she knew she mustn't seem too overpowering.

Conscious of his eyes upon her, she began to sing softly to herself as she slid the scones from the oven. Gorgeous. Baked to perfection. Happily she brewed the tea and packed a plate with the hot scones, butter, cream and jam.

'It's vile out,' she offered, passing him a plate.

'Unexpected. They forecast sun.'

To her secret pleasure he took two halves and healthy

dollops of everything to spread on top. She watched him out of the corner of her eye, wondering if last night had been unexpected for him, too.

'The path's an awful mess,' she ventured cheerfully.

'I've decided to have all the paths on the island properly laid. Gravel bed. York stone for the main one to the house.'

She beamed. 'Lovely. Scones all right?'

She wanted to giggle. The previous night they'd been as intimate as two people could be. Today they were politely chatting over a cream tea!

'Melting in the mouth.'

They contemplated one another's mouths for a moment before she was able to rouse herself and continue the silly conversation.

'How was Tokyo? Having a heatwave?' she asked brightly.

He looked puzzled. 'Oh. Tokyo. I don't know. I...I didn't do much work, actually.'

She lowered her lashes to hide her reaction. That was good, she thought in glee, her shaking hand making an awful mess of buttering the scone. She put it to one side and focused on calming herself down.

'Why was that?' she asked with pleasing indifference.

He took an intense interest in swirling his knife over the cream-topped scone and making intricate patterns.

'I want you to know,' he said heavily, 'that last night—'

'Yes?'

Her heart was racing. She couldn't sit there any longer so she got up and put some more wood into the belly of the stove.

'I hope you didn't get the wrong idea,' Zach muttered behind her. And she smiled, knowing she had the right idea even if he didn't recognise it. 'I did say before that you would be leaving—'

'In a month, yes,' she said evenly. And turned to smile at him.

He looked nonplussed. 'You...don't mind? I'm telling you that this...between us...is just a—'

'Fling,' she provided.

She had to turn away then, because he had looked wounded for a moment, before he'd brought those shutters over his pained eyes, and his inner disappointment had delighted her.

'Most women would be offended,' he growled.

'Ah, but I'm not most women.'

She returned to her seat, even more convinced that something fundamental had happened to him, too. Her eyes sparkled as she stretched out her arms to the fire and she felt, rather than saw, his silent intake of breath. And knew it was because he found her body exciting.

'Zach,' she murmured, wickedly hitching up her skirt, stretching out her legs to the stove and twiddling her toes in the cosy cartoon socks. 'I know the score. We made an agreement. What happened last night...' Her voice softened. 'It was wonderful. You are an incredible lover...' She felt her whole body go into meltdown at his mingled desire and shy pride. Oh, she adored him! 'But,' she continued a little shakily, 'I lead an independent life and I don't make demands on people. I'm not a clinger. I have too much pride for that. My philosophy is to take each day as it comes and to live that day to the full.'

She left the rest out. That the need to love and be loved was central to existence—and in Zach she had found the man who could fulfil her existence. The problem was to ensure he realised that too.

'That's fine,' he muttered.

But it didn't look fine at all. Lines of strain marred his mouth.

'Something wrong?' she asked gently.

'Headache. I have a lot of them. Hardly ever free.'

'I'm not surprised.'

He looked up at her sharply. 'What do you mean?'

'You are too hard on yourself. You don't give yourself enough leisure time. The body needs to rest. It needs peace and calm to regenerate itself.' She rose from the chair again. 'Where is the pain?'

'Here.' His fingers described a path from the root of his nose and over one brow to his temple.

Sitting on the arm of his chair, she gently reached out and stroked the deep crevasse between his eyebrows. After a moment's resistance he leaned back with a sigh.

'That's good,' he muttered.

'Stay there. I'll do it properly,' she said softly.

Deliberately she took her time adding lavender to the base oil. And she was very quiet, allowing the peaceful background music to soothe him in preparation.

To her surprise, she was nervous. But she wanted to ease his headache so very badly. She brought warm towels, gently easing one under his head and the other around his shoulders. Ideally she'd have him on the treatment bench, but that would be a step too far at the moment. Keep it casual. Spontaneous.

Putting all her love and tenderness into her movements, she began to massage his forehead. The tension there was alarming but it grew less and she could see his entire body gradually softening.

'Feels good,' he murmured, still, however, unconsciously fighting her touch.

Delicately she worked into his scalp with rhythmic, mesmerising movements. The lines on his face vanished, the muscles now in repose. And she felt a stab of awe at the change in him.

'How's that?' she asked tenderly.

He opened his eyes slowly, the thick, black lashes lifting like a curtain until he was gazing directly at her. A look of utter contentment passed between them.

'Wonderful,' he slurred.

She removed the towels and washed her hands. Then, with her heart in her throat, she went back to him. He pulled her on to his lap and, to her intense joy, he kissed her.

'Thank you.'

'My pleasure.'

'No. Mine.'

And he cuddled her to him, stroking her arm and occasionally kissing the top of her head. Deeply happy, Catherine curled her feet up and lay there, listening to the thudding of his heart. Gently he lifted her chin and brushed her lips with his.

'No strings.'

'None,' she whispered, and meant it.

Two people should be able to love in freedom, she thought dreamily, as his kisses deepened. She feared domination herself; had always shied away from the restrictions that some people seemed to put on one another the moment they became an 'item'. So she wasn't intending to make Zach her possession.

They made love and it was just as tender and intensely passionate as before. She felt very close to him and knew that they were now irretrievably linked.

'Tea's cold,' she murmured, when she finally began to emerge from her blissful daze.

'Come to the house tonight. I'll cook dinner,' he said

huskily and stroked her naked shoulder, then nibbled it appreciatively.

She captured his face in her hands and smiled at him, feeling infinitely happy.

'I'll come.'

Unable to resist his answering smile, she kissed its curves.

'Bring your toothbrush,' he said softly, and bent to kiss her in return. 'We can do our teeth in unison and admire the rainbows in the bathroom.'

'You like them?' she asked in delight.

'Love them.'

He stayed so long, just sitting there listening to the music and holding her in his arms, that they left for the manor and the promised dinner together.

Helping him to prepare the meal, she felt as though she were floating on air. Never had she been so happy.

'I *must* work tomorrow,' he murmured, ruffling her hair and suddenly kissing her ear as though he couldn't help but touch her.

'Of course. So must I.'

'Will you be free around tea-time?'

She rolled her eyes. 'You're after my scones again, aren't you?'

His mouth became wry. 'I'll probably need a massage too.'

'It's yours.'

And, she thought, padding over to check the pasta, so was she.

496   6037

CHAPTER TEN

TIME seemed to stand still. The days passed in a leisurely, golden glow. Living for each hour, she and Zach worked as usual then met up late every afternoon. And stayed together until morning.

But, although she felt as if she were bathed in sunlight every morning, the weather was actually unusually wet. Accordingly she had to abandon any idea of rubbing the rest of the boat down for its repaint job, and was obliged to put up with the scruffy door panels reproaching her.

Sam arrived each weekend and they spent wonderful, entire days together then, playing hide-and-seek in the house and other silly games.

Between rain showers they rushed out to check the pond for tadpoles and great crested newts, watching the nesting birds as they worked ceaselessly to feed their young.

They also added more and more outlandish items to the Den. To Catherine's joy, she, Zach and Sam behaved like crazy kids as they gradually turned it into a bizarre cross between a miniature stately home and an outlandishly tacky palace.

Their latest enthusiastic dawn trawl in the local markets and boot fairs had ended up with them triumphantly bearing home fake silver sprayed ornaments, gruesomely sentimental pictures of cats dressed as Victorians and a plaster statue so ugly that they could only marvel that it had ever been produced at all.

When they arranged their new finds with the rest of

what Zach loftily called their 'tat', they stood back in admiration and awe.

'Isn't it dreadful?' she cried in glee.

'Fantastically gross,' Zach said with a chuckle.

'Nobody's got a Den like this,' said Sam, pride and happiness bursting from every inch of him.

'I think you can be sure of that!' Zach agreed drily.

And they all collapsed in helpless laughter that left them weak and stretched out on the fake Persian carpet, its bilious greens and yellows so worn that in places the foam backing could be seen.

'This is heaven,' Catherine sighed blissfully when she could speak again.

Lying on his back, and in a position where the orange plastic chandelier could be viewed in all its glory, Zach reached out and squeezed her hand.

'Oh, I do hope not!' he groaned, and set them all laughing again.

With so much laughter in his life, Zach unwound a little more every day. That gave her more happiness than anything.

And she knew that she had fallen helplessly, irrevocably, head-over-heels in love with him.

They were all in the garden watching the swifts wheeling overhead one cloudy Sunday. She was explaining how the birds slept briefly on the wing but rarely landed.

Sam was fascinated. He wrote down the information in the nature notebook he'd begun to keep.

'They come all the way from Africa,' she told him. 'They go there for the winter, sensible birds.'

'They've got lovely slicy wings,' Sam remarked.

'The shape of a scimitar,' she agreed. 'A sword.'

'Oh, yes! I've seen those in cartoons,' Sam declared

eagerly. 'Why didn't we see the swallows yesterday? Have they only just arrived?'

'They were here last week. But today they're everywhere because it's cloudy and late in the day and the air is full of tiny flies. That's why they're so active. They're swooping about with their beaks wide open, sort of hoovering up flies as they go.'

'My goodness,' came a warm, female voice. 'I never knew that!'

'Mum!'

Sam leapt up to hug his mother as Catherine and Zach turned around.

Her heart bumped when Zach kissed his ex-wife fondly and asked how she was.

'I'm fine,' she said, eyeing him oddly. 'And you look well. What happened to your stressed-out look?'

'Dad doesn't work when I'm here,' Sam offered eagerly.

'That's a first,' Kate teased. Her thoughtful eyes swivelled to Catherine.

'This is Catherine Leigh.' Zach introduced them. 'And this is Kate, as you've probably gathered.'

'How do you do?' Catherine said, feeling a little wary. But Kate's smile was friendly, dispelling any awkwardness.

'I've heard nothing but "Catherine says," and "Catherine thinks," for the past few weeks!' she declared with a laugh.

'Oh. How embarrassing!' Catherine giggled.

'Not really. I've been envious of some of the things you've been doing. Could I possibly see this famous Den?' Kate asked.

Sam let out a squeal and dragged his mother off.

Catherine and Zach glanced at one another and meekly followed.

She decided she liked Kate very much. Although she was dressed casually, her clothes were obviously expensive. The linen suit and cashmere jumper were in a lovely muted cinnamon colour that showed off her glorious blonde hair, cut in a freely swinging bob.

Her manner with Sam was affectionate and un-mumsy and she listened to what her son said without any patronising smile or silly comments.

But it was her attitude to Zach—and his to Kate—that disconcerted Catherine. They teased one another. Touched. Exchanged the kind of looks that married people gave when their offspring were being particularly amusing, sweet, or cute.

Her heart began to beat hard. They were still linked, she thought, and tried to be pleased for Zach. She told herself that divorced people—who remained on good terms—would always have their child or children as a bond between them. And Kate was undeniably nice.

Why had they divorced? Were they still a little bit in love? If they'd parted because of Zach's hectic work schedule, would Kate fall for him all over again now that he was relaxed and human again?

Catherine felt cold inside. Kate and Zach had so much in common. And suddenly she was no longer sure of her future.

They went on to see her boat and Kate made all the right noises. Zach seemed eager to show his ex-wife how everything worked. And then the two of them began to chat in a friendly way.

Feeling something of an outsider, she retreated from the reminiscences and sat with Sam, watching the sun go down and turn the river to liquid gold.

'There you are, Sam!' declared Kate. 'I wondered where you'd got to. Daddy's asked us back for a drink.'

'You too, Catherine,' Zach said quietly.

'I think I'll stay here,' she said, feeling awkward. 'Don't want to intrude.'

'Nonsense. I insist. Please?' he said with a winning smile.

And with Sam and Kate adding their pleas she had no choice. Kate curled up in an armchair in the beautiful drawing room looking very much at home, while Catherine sat on the edge of a Victorian buttonback settee, feeling unusually nervous.

Sam settled himself at Catherine's feet, engrossed in writing up his nature notes and occasionally checking various points with her.

After an hour of answering Kate's questions about herself, Catherine felt exhausted. She wondered why she was getting the third degree.

'No, I don't feel lonely living on the boat,' she replied with as much patience as she could muster.

'Course not! You've got us!' Sam declared happily.

'Yuk!'

She wrinkled her nose in pretend distaste and Sam tussled with her. They ended up in a giggling heap on the floor. Catherine became aware of a faint frost emanating from Kate and hastily scrambled back to her seat.

Sam cuddled up to her and, after a moment's hesitation, she put her arm around the little boy. Kate might not like her son feeling affection for another woman but Catherine wasn't going to play it cool with him for Kate's sake.

'I have a whole heap of friends, you see,' she said calmly, answering the question rather belatedly.

'Heaps!' Sam marvelled. 'There's The Boys downriver who live in narrow boats too—and virtually everybody in the village. Everyone likes Catherine,' he declared loyally. 'She's mega.'

Zach's mouth curled in amusement. His eyes danced merrily at Catherine.

'Very popular,' he agreed.

'You must have a string of boyfriends, then,' Kate said with a smile that didn't quite reach her eyes.

'Only me!' giggled Sam, fortunately diverting attention from Zach's sudden stillness.

'Huh! You'll have to grow a bit before I'm walking down the aisle with you,' Catherine joked and Sam laughed.

'Yeah! We'd look a bit dopey!'

'So, lots of admirers?' persisted Kate.

Catherine could see that she was edgy.

'All The Boys want to marry her,' interjected Sam earnestly. 'I said I wanted to when I was grown up and they told me to get in line, buster.'

Catherine and Zach laughed and she hugged the solemn little boy.

'My goodness,' Kate murmured, her hand firmly on Zach's knee. 'We have a real Mata Hari here!'

'I think Sam's been exaggerating the extent of Catherine's relationships,' Zach muttered, looking annoyed.

'Some people who live on the fringe of society,' Kate said in a deceptively sweet voice, 'have different values, different ways of looking at relationships, to boring old fogies like you and me. You believe in freedom to do as you please, don't you, Catherine? I understand the appeal of that.'

She frowned. 'I like my freedom, yes.'

'There you are!' Kate turned triumphantly to Zach. 'A true free spirit. The open road—or, in this case, the open river—not a care in the world. Oh, it must be wonderful not to be burdened by responsibility. Or to feel obliged to stick to the dull courting rituals that society expects. The freedom to experiment and to share love with many people. It's very appealing, I can see that.'

'I hope you're not suggesting Catherine might be...' Zach glanced at Sam and considered his words carefully '...free with her favours?'

'Of course not!' Kate cried, looking horrified but clearly thinking exactly that. 'I was talking generally. I'm sure the...er...Boys...are moral and upright, despite appearances.'

'The Boys don't have the money to look smart,' Catherine explained, hoping to change the subject. 'And they're a mix of backgrounds, professions and ages—from twenty-two to fifty-three—'

'*Professions?*' Kate queried silkily.

'Oh, yes. Carpenters, decorators, plumbers and a silversmith,' Catherine replied quietly. 'They've been very kind to me. I suppose we're a close-knit community because we're boat people.'

Kate nodded. 'Same values.'

'We don't pursue money for its own sake,' Catherine agreed. She saw Zach's frown and decided to terminate the interrogation. 'Tomorrow they're all motoring up to an annual boat fair some distance away. I'll miss them,' she added unnecessarily. But it lightened the conversation. 'And now—' she rose decisively to her feet '—I really must go.'

'Oh, no!' protested Sam.

She hugged him and kissed his cheek. 'The Favs and Silver Laced's need me. See you next week. We'll check the weed hatch and paint the cabin slides we managed to rub down. OK?'

She turned to Kate with an understanding smile. It must be hard to see your kiddie so fond of someone else.

'Goodbye,' she said warmly, extending her hand. 'I'm glad we've met. Sam talks about you a lot.'

Kate's face became wreathed in smiles and Catherine's heart softened. The woman really did love her son.

'Does he? Don't believe all of it,' she joked. 'Goodbye, Catherine.'

'I'll see you out,' Zach drawled.

Sam scampered along with them. At the drawing room door Catherine half-turned on an impulse and caught Kate looking tight and upset. She bit her lip, wishing Kate felt more generous about her son's affections.

'Sam!' Kate called loudly. 'Come back and show me your nature book.'

For a moment he looked torn, and then with a gentle push from Catherine he galloped back to his mother.

'I'm glad you met Kate,' Zach murmured as they walked through the hall.

Yes, she thought. It was just as well that she knew as much as possible about Zach. Seeing Kate had raised doubts in her mind—and it was better to have those doubts now rather than later.

She decided to ask the questions which were burning inside her.

'Where did you meet her originally?'

'We both worked for the same financial house. We had a lot in common.'

She realised ruefully that she hadn't wanted to hear that.

'In that case, why did you two divorce?' she asked directly.

He shrugged. 'My fault entirely. I was devastated when

she said she wanted me to go. I thought I was doing everything right.'

'And weren't you?' she wondered.

'Not really. I started out with high ambitions and specific goals. I worked furiously to attain them so that my family was well-provided for and then, just as I was becoming established, my personal life collapsed. Kate was fed up with taking second place to my career. I am beginning now to see where I went wrong. It's all a question of balance, isn't it?' he said ruefully.

She managed a weak smile, squeezed his hand and pulled on her boots. Kate called Zach's name sharply. Hastily Catherine hurried out, turning with a farewell wave. But he had already gone back to his ex-wife and the door was firmly shut.

Catherine heaved a sigh. It seemed that her efforts to show Zach a less stressful way of life had reaped unexpected benefits for Kate, who now must be thinking that he was once again the man she'd fallen in love with.

Disconsolately she mooched about the boat, expecting to hear Kate's car starting up as she and Sam headed for their London home.

After two hours of tiptoeing around with her ears on full alert and hearing no such thing, Catherine decided she'd had enough. She'd go to the pub and cheer herself up with some friendly company.

The car was still there when she went over the bridge. It was still there when she returned at midnight, after a jolly evening and an hour or two chatting at a friend's home.

It was still there in the morning.

She hadn't meant to go and look, but something had driven her to do so. And when she saw the car was parked in exactly the same place her stomach swooped. For a moment she could hardly breathe as it dawned on her that they'd spent the night together.

Distraught, fighting with the ugliness of her jealousy, she went about her jobs mechanically. And felt a desperate need for her friends.

She had an excuse—not that she needed one. Her month's stay was virtually up and there seemed to be no chance that Zach would ask her to stay now that he and Kate were back on course. So she'd go to say goodbye to The Boys before they left for their trip.

Gloomily Zach watched Kate's car shoot off down the lane, touched when Sam appeared, half in and half out of the window, waving frantically. Yes, he thought, I must concentrate on my son. His needs are paramount.

The car slowed and he saw Sam's arms flapping again with renewed energy. This time the farewell wasn't for him. Zach's gaze swivelled to the group of boats moored to the bank, the focus of Sam's attention.

He stiffened. A familiar and slender figure on the big Dutch barge gracefully returned Sam's wave. For a moment Catherine stood there, holding hands with the curly-headed Tom who owned *Rainbow*. The two of them watched as Kate's car disappeared up the lane.

And then Zach froze. She had flung herself into Tom's arms. He felt rage boil within him and his rational mind battled to say it didn't matter, that he had no right to mind.

But they were cheek to cheek like lovers. It looked like he was kissing her. And a moment later they had disappeared into the cabin, glued together as though they'd been irretrievably welded by mutual adoration and hunger.

He had never felt such jealousy. It ripped through him so viciously that it stopped his breath. He rocked on his feet, totally submerged by a red hot anger and only his self-respect kept him from storming over to grab Tom and throw him in the river.

Was this the reason why Catherine had been so keen to keep their relationship on a 'no strings' basis? So that she could sleep with whoever she chose? It was none of his business how she lived her life.

But it hurt. So much that he could almost imagine that the lump in his throat and the moisture in his eyes was something to do with Catherine's betrayal, instead of the sharp wind that was now ruffling the river's surface.

Abruptly he turned around. Stumbled, half-blinded and numb, back to the house. Where he stood feeling totally lost and stupidly sorry for himself. But as angry as hell with Catherine.

A short time later he left for the City. It was all he could think of to do, with his mind so possessed by Catherine's casual treatment of his feelings.

Kate had rung him to say that she and Sam were safely home. He couldn't bring himself to tell Kate she'd been right about Catherine. That you couldn't live a life of freedom and not have some of it seep into your sex life.

And he had to admit that Catherine had been very nonchalant about their relationship. As far as she knew she was leaving in a week's time. And yet, even though she must have expected it would be a temporary fling, she had been more than willing to sleep with him.

She would never know that he'd been poised to suggest they make it a more permanent arrangement. His long conversation with Kate had saved him from a foolish mistake which he would have regretted for the rest of his life.

Angrily he punched in his first call. He was well out of it. Catherine was a butterfly, as Kate had said, and would never stay anywhere long enough. It wasn't in her nature. You couldn't tame a half-wild creature or change its ways. How stupid of him to think he could.

He could have kicked himself for being taken in. Not once, in the whole of his life, had he ever been gullible. But Catherine had softened him up and offered him so many delights…

His body flamed while his heart ached. And, determined not to be ruined by the loss of the enchanting but fickle Catherine, he planned a week of back-to-back meetings.

Annoyingly, work gave him little pleasure. He found his attention wandering sometimes, occasionally while he was in mid-sentence but particularly when one of his employees was earnestly holding forth.

All too often his mind leapt longingly to the island with its leafy calm and amusing dabchicks. To a woman with her hair tumbling about her as she raised her arms to him and purred with satiated lust.

'Zach? Are you with me?'

He blinked at the fresh-faced, sharp-eyed young man in the regulation city suit, two inches of cuff and an attitude of ferocious ambition. That was him, ten years ago. Ten long years of working from seven in the morning till eleven at night. Would this young man end up with a broken marriage too?

He frowned, realising that everyone around the table was looking alarmed, as if they suspected he'd lost the plot.

'Where else would I be?' he growled. 'Get to the point.'

Where else? On an island. Bedding a treacherously amoral woman who had no idea that it might hurt people if she offered her favours around. For all his macho image, he knew he was a deeply moral man. That was his parents' influence. He'd squired women around since his divorce but hadn't slept with any of them.

He wanted a loving wife who'd accept Sam as her own. More children. A welcoming home, where the smell of newly baked bread and children's laughter offered him a haven from life.

And Catherine would never have filled that role.

He nodded approvingly at the young tyro and the meeting broke up in a rustle of papers and the sound of laptops being closed. His staff respected him. Looked up to him.

Little did they know that he'd just had his first affair and he'd retired from it severely wounded!

The week passed. He was unnervingly reluctant to get up each morning and drag himself through the crowded city to work. Felt resentful. Became irritated by Kate's incessant calls. So he pushed himself harder and hated every minute of every day.

Whenever he gazed out at the rain-lashed grey pavements of central London he wondered what the devil he was doing there. And felt a rush of homesickness for his beautiful island.

By the time he'd driven through massive traffic jams in the teeming rain and was back at the Manor for Sam's weekend visit, he'd become thoroughly bad-tempered. What he needed was a massage. Without any strings attached.

His mood didn't improve when Kate rang to say that Sam had gastro-enteritis and would be staying at home.

'Why don't you come over? Stay the weekend?' she suggested warmly.

'Better not,' he said with frustrated regret. 'It's passed on by contact, isn't it? I don't want to risk passing on anything like that to my secretary. She's pregnant. I'll call him, have a chat.'

'Sam will be so disappointed,' sighed Kate. 'And me. Incidentally, I was wondering how he got it. Have you or Catherine had any stomach upsets at all?' she asked lightly.

'I wouldn't know about her. I've been in London all week and I've been fine,' he muttered, annoyed that his eagerly anticipated weekend had been scuppered.

'Oh, well,' Kate said, sounding cheerful. 'I suppose she's got used to germs, the way she lives.'

She rang off before he could remind her that, however grubby Catherine's morals might be, her narrow boat was perfectly clean and tidy.

Uncertain whether to go or stay, he spent the next hour lethargically stopping a leak in the wall of the utility room. Perhaps it was the unearthly silence of the empty house, but the rain sounded very loud outside and the noise of the river seemed more like Niagara than the serene Saxe. It was, however, too dark and foul outside for him to go and look.

He settled himself in the drawing room with a post-dinner brandy—the meal being a miserable apology of a packaged lamb casserole and assorted E numbers which would have appalled Catherine.

Pity she didn't seem to have the same exacting standards where her body was concerned.

Looking up to glower at the teeming rain, he saw a light wobbling about outside in the garden. He leapt to his feet, his heart beating hard. When he reached the window and peered out he saw a shadowy figure with a torch, rooting about in one of the outbuildings.

His mouth compressed. One of those Boys, scavenging. He should have put in those security lights and an alarm system. Catherine had soothed his suspicions about The

Boys, and because of that he hadn't sent his art works away for safety.

Nevertheless, he suspected that The Boys' sense of property wasn't as rigid as his and they'd take anything they regarded as of little value. Unless, he thought stiffening, it was a real burglar.

Grimly he strode to the kitchen and pulled out his new boots, only to be brought up sharp by a frantic rapping on the door. It shook on its hinges as someone tried to turn the handle.

Burglars didn't announce their presence. Nevertheless, he grabbed a carving knife and unbolted the door. A small, bedraggled figure tumbled in.

'Catherine!' Discarding the knife he caught her, held her up, and as he did so his hands actually squeezed water from her sopping jumper. He felt an odd kind of fury. 'You *fool* to come out without a coat in this!'

'Oh, shut up, Zach! I need a rope!' she screamed hysterically, her face contorted in panic.

'A rope? What the devil for?' he demanded.

She drew in a shuddering breath. *'My boat's sunk!'* she wailed.

CHAPTER ELEVEN

FOR a fraction of a second he stared at her in astonishment. Then he pushed her roughly into a chair.

'Sit there!' he ordered grimly. 'And don't move a muscle!'

Racing upstairs three at a time, he roared along to the linen cupboard and grabbed two bath towels before charging back again at breakneck speed.

'Get your clothes off,' he snapped. 'Wrap up in these—'

'No!' she yelled, leaping up and banging the table in helpless frustration. 'Didn't you hear me? My boat's sunk—!'

'What do you think you're going to do about it?' he said impatiently. 'Lasso it and drag it up again?'

'Secure it!' she hurled, her entire body shaking as if she had a fever. 'Stop it being dragged downstream!'

'You're doing no such thing. Get out of those wet clothes. Take a warm bath and root about in my wardrobe till you find something that'll fit you,' he ordered. '*I'll* secure your damn boat.'

'But—'

'See sense, Catherine!' he barked, irrationally bad-tempered with her. 'We're wasting time here and every second counts. I'm stronger than you and I know enough about boats to manage. Now do as you're told.'

He didn't wait for her to argue, but togged himself up in his new waterproofs and picked up a powerful searchlight. There was a towing rope in the shed—he'd seen it when they'd been watching the swallows building their nests there.

The rain had mercifully died down. When he got to the bank with the rope he saw that the river had risen at least seven feet or so. And there, straddled across the raging torrent with its stern wedged on the opposite bank, was Catherine's boat.

Or, at least, five feet of it. The rest was beneath the water, dragged down at a perilous angle by the bow rope which was still attached to its mooring somewhere beneath the surging river.

It was surprising that Catherine should have been so careless and unobservant that she hadn't eased off the mooring ropes. Perhaps she'd been otherwise occupied with a lover or two.

A flash of fury ripped through him and he had to force himself to concentrate on the task in hand. To secure the stern he'd have to get to the other bank. That meant a long walk to the village, crossing the weir there, and walking back down the other side.

But he managed it. Scrabbled down the muddy bank, fixed the rope and tied it securely to a stout tree. Panting with exertion he arrived back at the house a good hour and a half later.

Catherine was huddled over the stove, frail and frightened and almost lost inside one of his warm shirts and a jumper. A pair of his socks flopped oddly on her small feet and he felt a jerk of something tender and painful in his chest.

'All done,' he said crossly, shedding his wet boots and coat. With curt thanks, he took the towel she offered. He rubbed at his wet hair. 'Brandy for you—'

'I've had some. I hope you don't mind,' she said in a

small voice. 'I got you a glass, too. You've been ages. I thought…I thought—'

'I crossed the river,' he snapped, accepting the drink and cradling it in his hands. 'It took a while.'

'I wish I'd come with you,' she mumbled.

Her eyes were huge and panicky, her mouth trembling. And she'd been crying. Every inch of his stupid, treacherous body yearned to console her. Appalled, he took a sip of the brandy and felt revived.

'You wouldn't have been able to do anything and you would have been in the way,' he said shortly. 'At least you can be sure that your boat won't go anywhere now. We can't do any more till morning. Sit down, for goodness' sake. You look terrible. Tell me what happened.'

'I don't really know, except I think someone must have opened the sluice gates,' she mumbled. 'The first I knew was that the boat was rocking wildly and it seemed to be rising up.'

'That makes sense. The river's several feet higher than usual. It looked like the water at the base of Niagara— boiling white waves surging in all directions.' He looked down at her and suddenly found himself giving impromptu thanks for her preservation. 'I don't know,' he said gruffly, 'how you ever escaped.'

She shuddered. 'Sheer luck. If I'd been in bed…'

His hand touched her shoulder briefly and she gave him a brave little smile which ripped into his heart more surely than if she'd burst into tears.

Don't be swayed, he told himself. Don't weaken.

'You're here. You're safe.' He gave a dismissive wave of his hand as though the whole event had been a minor incident.

Her eyes looked hollow. 'I know. I don't know how. I'll never forget it.'

She stared into space, reliving the horrific moment. He felt desperate to know every detail. But in asking would he betray his concern? He could see her going over and over it all, her hands trembling uncontrollably. And he could contain himself no longer.

'You must tell me,' he said in the manner of a detached counsellor, pulling up a chair in front of her. 'Don't keep it bottled up,' he advised loftily. 'Run through the events.'

Her hand swept over her tumbled curls. 'It was so quick!' she marvelled. 'I was trying to keep my balance as the boat heeled over. In a matter of seconds there was a loud rushing sound outside and all the timbers sort of…groaned.' She bit her lip.

Zach's muscles strained with the effort of containment. He folded his arms to keep them from reaching out.

'Go on,' he said coolly.

She was too wrapped up in what had happened to notice his detachment. 'I could hear the ropes squeaking, that's the only word that describes it,' she mumbled. 'I flung open the stern doors to see walls of white water rushing at me. It was foaming over the stern. I don't know why, but instinctively I leaped for the bank—just as the stern mooring gave way with the force of the river.' She shuddered. 'The tree must have been literally torn from the bank. I stood there, clinging on for dear life as the water rose around my feet and watched my boat being dragged across the river. I saw most of it disappear under the water. For a long time I couldn't move. I kept thinking I could have been drowned!' she wailed.

He covered up his horror and steeled himself not to comfort her physically. Words would have to do. Otherwise he'd abandon the promise he'd made to himself that he'd not get involved with Catherine again.

'Yes. But you weren't. You're just shocked.' He saw

that her fingers kept plucking at her skirt and her knees still shook. 'Catherine,' he said in what he thought was a more fatherly tone. 'You are alive. That's the main thing. Nothing else matters. Your life is more important than any possessions. They can be salvaged or acquired again. *You* are *alive*,' he repeated passionately. 'It's a blessing.'

'Yes,' she croaked. 'You're right. I am lucky. I'm holding on to that.'

'Good,' he encouraged. 'As for someone opening those sluice gates, I think it's outrageous they should do that without warning anyone downstream,' he fumed, reaching for the telephone directory. 'We must both sue, of course. There must have been thousands of gallons released in a matter of minutes. Whoever opened those sluices—'

'It's my home,' she said, her plaintive voice interrupting his rant. 'Everything I love and own. It'll all be ruined—even if I ever manage to raise her. All my medicating potencies, my patient records— Oh, excuse me!' she flared, seeing him punching numbers into his mobile phone. 'Have I interrupted an international conference call or something?'

'I'm calling the emergency number of the Water Board,' he replied tightly.

How could she think that? he thought, furious that she could imagine he'd be so crass.

'Oh, I'm *sorry*! I don't know what I'm saying, my mind's jerking about all over the place—'

He flung her a glance of contempt that stopped her apology in its tracks. Someone answered his call. He began to lodge his complaint with the official. After listening to the man's explanation, he put the phone down.

'Nobody sanctioned the release of the sluice gate,' he told Catherine curtly. 'The officer thinks it must have been vandals. Were you insured?'

Her look of dismay gave him the answer and he felt like shaking her till her teeth rattled.

'Don't glare at me like that!' she wailed. 'I was going to!'

'Honestly, Catherine,' he snapped in exasperation. 'You take casual living too far! You have to take responsibility more seriously. You've made yourself homeless!'

Cringing from his tongue-lashing—which he secretly knew came from despair at the vast differences between them—she incoherently mumbled an excuse.

'I know! But the insurance had come up for renewal. I...I was waiting till I'd found somewhere else and could give the new mooring site,' she said miserably. 'It—it seemed to make sense at the time.'

She looked so forlorn that he almost caught her up in his arms and told her that he'd buy her a new boat. But he managed to stop himself before he lost his head.

He remained silent and brooding. There was nothing to say. No consolation to offer. She had lost her home, her entire possessions and her means of making a living.

'I wish The Boys were here,' she mourned.

He winced, his male pride wounded. 'Why?' he flung back.

Her dark, passion-filled eyes flashed up to his.

'Because they'd know how to raise her! Then they'd show me how to take the boat apart and dry it and...'

'I could do that,' he found himself saying to his horror.

The shining light in her eyes completely erased any thoughts he might have had of giving a light laugh and saying that he'd been talking rubbish. And then her face fell.

'You can't know much about raising a boat,' she said glumly.

His mouth hardened. 'I'm not incapable,' he said with

icy frostiness. 'It's all a matter of common sense and ap-
plication. I have a good brain, some practical knowledge
and plenty of people I can draw on for advice. Of course
I can do it,' he scoffed.

The hopeful light shone in her eyes again. 'Could you?'
she asked eagerly. 'There might be a chance I can salvage
stuff if it's not under water too long.'

He scowled, just to make sure she knew he wasn't doing this because he wanted to pick up their relationship
again.

'I don't have much choice,' he growled. 'I don't want
the wretched boat blocking the river, do I?'

She looked suitably chastened. 'No. But…the fire bri-
gade won't be able to get to the site. Nor would a crane.
And The Boys aren't around. I don't see how you could
raise her on your own. I suppose we'll have to ask some
of my village friends to help—'

'Do they know anything about boats?' he asked.

'No, but they'd be willing—'

'If they're not used to the river and boats they'll be
more hindrance than they're worth, however well-
meaning they might be. I can't spare time and energy to
watch over their safety and keep telling them what to do.
Better we cope on our own. I'll get her up,' he promised
recklessly. 'And we'll salvage what we can.'

'Zach, I would be so grateful!' she whispered.

'I want the river clear,' he repeated. Not wanting her
to offer herself in return. He beetled his brows together.
'It's very annoying. You were due to go.'

She bit her lip and hung her head. 'Yes. I'm sorry. I
couldn't know this was going to happen, though.'

'No. I appreciate that.'

Hell. She looked so forlorn. Restlessly he strode up and
down, fighting the overwhelming urge to give her a hug.

'Well.' He heard her get to her feet. Heard the misery and shock that robbed her voice of its gentle serenity. 'We can't do anything now. I'd better find somewhere to stay,' she muttered.

He whirled around to see her trudging disconsolately to the door.

'Don't be ridiculous. You'll stop here.'

With her back to him she paused, her shoulders drooping.

'You don't want me around. I don't think so,' she said tightly.

'I'm not intending to haul you into my bed,' he grated, crushing the stab of pain that had arrowed into his heart. She didn't want his consolation. Was scared that he'd make sexual demands on her. Presumably her affections had swung to Tom for the moment. And who might it be next week? Fury ripped through him. Or perhaps it was pain. Difficult to tell. 'There are plenty of bedrooms without me having to invite you into mine,' he snapped, cut to the quick by her fickle nature.

She had gone scarlet. 'It's… I can't impose on you,' she stumbled.

'I don't want you in this house, any more than you want to be,' he told her coldly. 'But it makes sense. You'll be on hand in the morning to see the damage. There's no point in finding digs in the village at this time of night. See sense, Catherine!' he fumed, when she didn't respond. 'If you think I'm going to jump you, then you're out of your mind! I've moved on from our *fling*.'

'Yes. Of course,' she said tiredly. 'Thank you. I would be grateful. I feel so shaky I can hardly move.'

'Go to bed, then. I'll show you up and find some linen.'

She winced at his curtness. Hell, he thought. He really was giving her a hard time. She'd nearly drowned, had lost her entire home and everything she possessed, and he was barking at her as if she'd done something wrong.

'Catherine…' he began, more softly.

'Don't worry!' Aroused by an extraordinary passion, she glared at him, her dark eyes blazing into his. 'I won't be a nuisance, if that's what you're concerned about. In fact, you don't need to help at all. I can do this on my own. I don't need you. Except for a bed tonight. And, since I'm leaving in three days, Kate won't know I've stayed the night, either, because I won't be around to tell her—and I'm sure you won't!'

Puzzled, he stared after her as she set off for the hall. She was distraught, she didn't know what she was saying. He followed her taut, stomping figure up the stairs, aching to gather her into his arms and soothe her till she fell asleep from sheer exhaustion. But he kept his barriers up, even though he longed to tear them down.

He and Catherine were worlds apart. They'd fused in bed for a brief time. But that wasn't enough.

'Have this room,' he said irritably, dumping pillows and sheets in the main guest bedroom.

'Thanks. I'm sorry to be a nuisance.'

He grunted. She took one corner of the sheet. Between them they made the bed in total silence. She seemed as tense and as wound up as he was, but then she'd lost her home and everything in it.

'Anything else you want?' he enquired coolly, anxious to leave before his self-discipline cracked.

'No. Thank you.' Her head lifted and he saw a new resolve in her expression. 'Zach, I meant what I said. I can do this on my own.'

He felt an enormous respect for her then. She was forcing herself to overcome the shock and, instead of giving way to perfectly understandable tears, she was beginning to fight the calamity that had befallen her.

'But I will help, whether you like it or not,' he said gruffly. 'I have no intention of having that river jammed by your boat for days on end. We'll talk in the morning. Try to sleep.'

Catherine woke with a start after finally falling asleep in the early hours. Her mind had teemed with thoughts and, try as she might, she hadn't been able to settle down.

She was homeless, she thought, the horror washing icily through her body. And even though she cared little for possessions, the few she had were important to her.

Nausea churned in her stomach. She'd never been in such an awful situation.

As she slipped on Zach's shirt she wondered how long it would be before she could earn her living again. And...in the meantime, where would she live?

Trying to be positive, to remind herself that she was fit and young—and alive—she tiptoed down the stairs to see if her clothes had dried where she had hung them over the Aga.

She paused in the kitchen doorway, her face softening with tenderness. There was Zach, fast asleep and slumped over the pine table with his head on his arms, his faithful mobile and sheaves of paper close by.

Her eyes hardened. He'd been catching up on work that she'd interrupted. She thought of his coldness the night before, his reluctance to even pat her shoulder in sympathy. She'd longed for a gesture from him.

But his manner had made it perfectly clear what he felt about her now—*nothing*. Anger surged through her, making her eyes blaze. Why couldn't he have told her he was back with Kate? Was it because he saw their *fling* as something utterly inconsequential?

Her blood boiling, she moved closer. But she saw that instead of working on financial figures and percentages he'd clearly been organising the delivery of industrial pumps, a winch and a canoe. And some of the pages were covered with calculations.

It seemed that he'd been up all night, puzzling over methods of raising her boat. Instead of being pleased, she felt upset. Her mouth tightened. He must be desperate to get rid of her!

Feeling horribly depressed by this, she left him sleeping while she hurriedly dressed in the utility room and then slipped out to check on the chickens. The door banged when she returned and he woke with a start, staring at her with a blank expression.

'Sorry. I didn't mean to disturb you,' she said stiffly.

He groaned and ran a hand over his sleepy face. She saw that his cheek bore marks from the creases of his sleeve and her heart softened for a moment before she angrily reclaimed it again. He groaned more loudly when he checked his watch.

'Is that the time? I meant to be up early.' Stiff and awkward, he got up and stretched his cramped body, his eyes narrowing. 'You've been out,' he accused.

'To see the chickens. Why shouldn't I?' she defended with a toss of her head. 'And you can bill me if you like for the bread I pinched to feed them. You'll be glad to know they're fine. They spent all night roosting in the trees.'

'You can have the bread with my compliments,' he said caustically. 'What about the boat?'

'Still there. Your mooring held.' She hesitated, her manners overcoming her anger with him. 'It was a dangerous thing to do,' she said jerkily. 'I—I can't thank you enough—'

'We've got to get that boat up so you can take it off to be repaired,' he said curtly.

Catherine felt as if he'd stamped on her. She was a nuisance in his eyes. And an embarrassment. He would move heaven and earth to get rid of her. He must know that Kate wouldn't be too pleased to have another woman around when she and Sam came to live with Zach again.

'First it has to be raised,' she said, her spirits sunk as deeply as her boat. 'Maybe it can't be repaired. I don't know how I'll afford to do so, anyway.'

'It will have to be raised. I'm not having it here. I'll show you what I've organised.' Cold and grim-mouthed, he waved a curt hand at the papers on the table. 'I'll go up for a shower and get dressed. Perhaps you'd do us some breakfast. We'll need a good meal inside us.'

She nodded glumly. He was doing his best to ensure that she didn't jump to any conclusions about the help he was giving her. Every gesture, every detached remark, were designed to keep her at arm's length. When she wanted to be hugged and stroked. To hear his warm, rich voice murmuring that everything would be all right.

She wanted to cry. She had never felt so isolated or alone in the whole of her life.

Her head lifted as she remembered something and she called to him as he left the kitchen.

'Zach! It's the weekend!'

'So?'

She hesitated, upset that the raising of her boat would be put off. But he had priorities. Sam and Kate.

'You'll want to be spending it with Sam—'

'He's not well. Tummy bug,' he answered curtly.

'Poor kiddie!' she sympathised. 'You...you don't have

to help me,' she said, denying her own needs. Sam was sick. He'd want to see his father. 'Your Sam is more important—'

'I know he is. But my secretary is pregnant and I wouldn't want her to catch the bug from me. It's better I keep away. He's sleeping most of the time anyway.'

She gazed at his closed face and wished she could see into his mind.

'You won't see Kate…' she ventured, unable to help herself.

'No,' he said, frowning, and he turned abruptly on his heel and disappeared.

Catherine swallowed back the lump in her throat. With a huge effort she pulled herself together and started grilling bacon. They would be working closely together over the next few hours. If she was to survive without wincing with the pain of 'if only' every time he came near, she'd better shape up and get used to the fact that Zach had been reclaimed by his ex-wife.

It would be good for Sam to have his parents back together, she consoled herself. But, try as she might, she couldn't accept that it would be good for Zach. She hung her head. That was very selfish of her. And arrogant to think that only she could make him happy.

Tears tried to water down the eggs she was scrambling. Furiously she scrubbed at her eyes with her handkerchief, vowing that she would be tough from now on. She had a mountain to climb in terms of her future. A boat to renovate, a life to begin all over again. The future seemed utterly daunting and unfriendly.

There wasn't any place for emotion. She choked back a sob. No place at all.

CHAPTER TWELVE

By the time Zach hurtled back into the kitchen again she was calm and determined. Quickly she drew their breakfasts from the simmer oven and slid them on to the table.

'Right,' she said briskly, picking up her knife and fork. 'Tell me what you've organised. You clearly spent half the night ringing people. Weren't they all in bed?'

'I called colleagues in New York who put me on to experts,' he replied. 'They explained what I had to do. I worked out the maths. We need three industrial pumps and a winch with a grappling hook if we're to pull the boat off that bank. Because the mud will be soft, the stern will be firmly embedded by now. The cabin has to be sealed entirely if the pumping is to be efficient. That can be done today—I doubt we'll be able to get hold of the pumps themselves till tomorrow at the earliest. I'll get on with sealing the boat while you make the phone calls.'

She was impressed. 'I want to help you,' she said quickly. 'I want to be there. You shouldn't be working on your own out there. Anything might happen.'

He considered this for a moment, his cold Arctic eyes boring right through her.

'You're right,' he said eventually. 'Take my mobile in case of emergency, and keep me in sight.'

As he explained what he intended to do she was helpless to prevent the admiration showing in her eyes. Cool and efficient, Zach was taking charge. And she knew that he would succeed because he had an air of total confidence in himself.

It wasn't misplaced, either. Watching his increasingly animated face and listening to his crisp, well-ordered plan, she began to realise that he was an extraordinary combination of practicality and intelligence.

Her eyes grew wider and wider. Her secret love for him spilled out and it must have reached him because he stopped in mid-sentence and looked confused, as if he'd lost the thread of what he'd been saying.

'I'm sorry,' she whispered, hot from the fierce tension in the room. 'Go on.'

He cleared his throat. All she could do was gaze at him, weak with love. Like an embarrassed uncle, he patted her hand and stood up.

'It'll be all right,' he said in his familiar, abrupt manner. 'Rely on me. I know exactly what I'm doing.'

She wished she knew what *she* was doing. Whatever common sense told her, it seemed that her heart and soul were conspiring to rebel. She wanted to be with Zach. Till the end of her life.

But she made an effort to block out her needs. However badly he'd behaved, his needs were more important. If he loved Kate, then she had to accept that. She ought to be glad that a broken marriage was being mended and a little boy would have both his parents back again.

After pushing the dishes into the dishwasher she listened silently to her instructions. Obediently she searched the telephone book for the numbers she wanted and then went out to make her calls from the riverbank as Zach had suggested.

That evening they staggered back exhausted. Only the darkness had stopped Zach from continuing. She supported his stumbling, weary body, marvelling at his dogged determination.

'You need a bath,' she murmured, aching with love.

He almost crawled up the stairs. She ran his bath and looked at him, slumped on a stool, his hair dripping from where he'd dived over and over again—in just a pair of bathing trunks—to secure a tarpaulin around the boat.

She had been terrified when he'd said it was the only way to seal the various outflow pipes. When he'd disappeared beneath the boat to drag the tarpaulin through to the other side, she had known that if he didn't surface soon then she'd jump in after him. And she would get him out, or die in the attempt.

Her love awed her. She would willingly die for him, she knew. Would Kate?

Reproaching herself for that question, she gently began to undress him.

'I can do that,' he croaked, rousing himself and irritably pushing her away.

'I'll bring you something to eat,' she said softly, ignoring his bad temper.

'You must be tired too,' he muttered, slowly and painfully shrugging off his wet shirt.

His laboured movements brought a tenderness to her eyes. 'I haven't done half as much work. I haven't fixed panels of wood over smashed windows and doors. I haven't spent half the day under water. I didn't heave things out of the boat, either. You wouldn't let me.'

'Everything was submerged. You'd never have had the strength,' he grunted. 'I only got out the chairs and other bulky things. I thought they'd get in the way tomorrow.'

'I know.' She stroked his forehead, wanting to erase his frown. 'Zach,' she murmured.

He seemed to tense up. And he turned his head away as if in disgust. 'I'm too tired to talk,' he muttered.

'I just wanted to say thank you,' she persisted. 'Whatever your reasons, you've been wonderful. I mean that, Zach. From the bottom of my heart. Thank you.'

With pain in her heart she went down to heat a tin of soup, all she felt she could manage to prepare. Wearily she took it up to his room. He fell asleep as soon as he'd finished and she lightly caressed his forehead, knowing that this would probably be the last time she'd be able to be so close to him.

His lashes, so thick and dark and lush on his cheeks, gave a little flutter. Her fingers stilled.

'Don't stop,' he murmured.

'I should go,' she breathed, feeling unnervingly weak.

Languidly the smoky eyes opened. 'You're swaying on your feet. And you're trembling.'

'I think the shock is beginning to tell,' she admitted in a whisper.

Her legs buckled and she steadied herself with a hand on the bed.

'I've been hard on you,' he said in a low voice.

'You—you've done more than anyone could have asked,' she said jerkily.

She couldn't tear her eyes away. And she found herself shaking so much that she couldn't remove her hand when he placed his over it, his face dark with concern.

He was worried she'd be a burden, she thought dejectedly. That she might hang around, pleading poverty and desperation, and might queer his pitch with Kate. A sob jerked out from her trembling lips.

'Here,' he grated roughly. 'Lie down for a minute. You're dead on your feet.'

She swayed, fighting her longing to agree. 'I—I can't—'

'Don't flatter yourself,' he muttered. 'I have no designs on you. But I'm too tired to carry you to the other room and you're in a terrible state and incapable of going under your own steam. Get in.' He eased back the bedclothes and moved to the far edge. 'Plenty of room. Lie down and let's both get some rest,' he added irritably. 'I don't want to spend half the night arguing. I've had enough.'

It seemed she had no fight left in her. So she slid into the bed and lay there, shaking with exhaustion, shock and misery.

After a moment, Zach heaved an exasperated sigh and none too gently pulled her to him. Immediately her body sank gratefully into his. Muscle by muscle, she gradually relaxed.

Cuddled into the warmth of his body she heard his deep breathing and felt glad that he was getting some rest. It was going to be tough the next morning.

Tough for him because of the physical work he had ahead of him. Tough for her because she'd be waking up in the knowledge that soon Kate would be in this bed, right here. Kate would be making love to him, sighing, dying with joy beneath his caresses and gasping with pleasure at his whispered words of love.

Despite her silence, something woke him and he turned over, his hands searching for her face in the dark. When his fingers slid over her tear tracks, he gave a low cry of compassion.

'Catherine,' he soothed, holding her close. 'Don't cry. It will all be fine. I promise.'

She knew then that he imagined she was sobbing over her boat and her homelessness. She didn't correct him. He was kissing away her tears and she couldn't bear it.

Her mouth closed on his and immediately fire flowed through her veins. Far from being tired, she felt she could conquer the world. But suddenly he pushed her away, as if he'd only just realised what he was doing.

'We need to sleep,' he muttered.

'Yes,' she jerked out hastily. 'I'm shattered.'

And she turned her back on him, burning with hunger and humiliation because she'd made a fool of herself. Again.

The pumps arrived—she discovered later—at six the next morning. Zach was up and out before she even stirred, which was just as well because she was glad of some time to gather herself before she faced him.

Wearing the survival suit she'd ordered, Zach was feeding the flexible pump hoses into one of the tiny windows at the stern of the boat, the only part above water.

She knew what she had to do. He'd explained the day before. When she'd finished feeding the chickens, Zach slid into the inflatable canoe and took her over to the boat.

She clambered on to the cabin roof and waited by the pumps while he disappeared into the submerged cabin. Then in response to his shout, she switched the pumps on and arcs of water gushed out into the river.

For a long time nothing seemed to be happening. Every now and then, when the water became a trickle, she slammed her hand as he'd directed over the pump outlets to let suction build up again. After two tiring hours, she realised that she could see more of the roof. Her relief was immense. The boat must be rising!

When Zach emerged to check on progress she crawled to the edge of the roof in excitement and looked down at his elated face.

'It's working!' she cried, overjoyed.

'Yeah. Slowly but surely!' he shouted happily. 'Keep it going. Nice work.'

'Oh, Zach!' she yelled. 'Look! It's Tom's boat! He's back!'

His mouth tightened when he saw the big Dutch barge heading towards them and Tom's appalled face peering from the cockpit.

'Get him on to the pumps,' Zach said curtly. And disappeared back inside.

Her delight at seeing Tom had put him in his place. He took a deep breath and dived beneath the water in the cabin, his raw and bleeding fingers ripping spoons, paper, reeds and muck from the wire covering the pump nozzles so that they weren't blocked.

He concentrated on that. The pain was almost welcome. The cold seeped into his bones despite the survival suit and he was about to scramble out of the rear cabin doors when he bumped into a familiar figure in the boatsman's cabin.

'Hot coffee's on the go,' Tom announced cheerily. 'Doughnuts, too. You look bushed. Take a break.'

He was about to decline the offer when he realised he was being stupid. A good shot of caffeine would be very welcome, even if he had to drink it while Tom and Catherine gazed into one another's eyes.

'Thanks,' he said gratefully, following the curly-haired Tom.

They sat on the Dutch barge while Catherine described what had happened. Zach was relieved that she showed no inclination to snuggle up to her boyfriend.

In fact, anyone would have been forgiven for imagining that her main concern was for Zach himself, since she cried out in distress when she saw his bloodied fingers.

'If I had my equipment I could have treated them,' she wailed, holding his injured hands in dismay.

'I'd rather have a warm jumper,' he said wryly. 'I'm freezing.'

'I'll get one. OK, Tom?' she asked, half-way to the cabin door.

'You know where they are,' he said amiably. 'And would you bring out the whisky? We'll have a tot in our coffees.'

Zach frowned at his knees and wished he hadn't asked. How many more men's wardrobes did she know intimately? he wondered angrily.

He accepted the dash of whisky and downed his drink then took Tom's sweatshirt from her. With muttered thanks he unzipped the survival suit and wriggled out of the upper half, pulling on the cosy top and zipping himself up again.

'I'm going back,' he said tersely and before she or Tom could say anything he had dived back into the river to check the boat's timbers.

Slowly, over the next few hours, the water receded in the cabin till it was only up to his knees. It had left a terrible trail of destruction. Mud and silt was everywhere, from the ceiling to the floor and in every nook and cranny. He looked at Catherine's precious books and despaired. Beneath the murky water he could see that the heavy tomes which held her patients' records had slid to the floor. They were thick with sludge and completely saturated.

Some things like the cutlery, cooking pans and plates could be steam cleaned. Her bedding would have to be thrown away. But other items were irreplaceable. Would all her photos, books and documents have to be dumped?

He wanted to be the one who comforted her when she saw the mess. But it would be Tom, of course. Hugging. Kissing. Murmuring sweet nothings—

'Hi.'

His head jerked around. 'Hi, Tom,' he said, trying to get his voice right.

'Came to help. Catherine insisted. She said your fingers would be down to the bone otherwise.'

'Thanks.'

He hated himself. He'd been imagining Tom as his enemy. But common sense told him that this guy, now in waders and oilskins and energetically clearing the nozzles of debris, must be gentle and kind. Catherine wouldn't have slept with him otherwise.

'Steve and Nick are manning the pumps,' Tom shouted above the noise of the pump motors. 'Dudley's making one of his famous curries. We've sent Catherine back to help.'

He looked into Tom's open, genial face and found himself regretting his jealousy. Contrary to his earlier belief, Tom was a hard worker and they made a good team. So he smiled and nodded and they went back to work companionably till only a puddle or two of water sloshed about in the boat.

'What a nightmare! She'll be devastated,' Tom said quietly, looking around at the chaos.

Zach took a step and felt the water squelching in the cavity beneath the tongue and groove floor.

'This'll have to come up. All the wood panelling on the sides, too.' His heart felt heavy. 'She won't accept financial help, I suppose.'

'No.' Tom looked worried. 'Unfortunately we're all off again tomorrow.'

Startled, Zach straightened his aching back. 'She'll need you,' he said selflessly. 'Can't you stay?'

'Not this time.' Tom grinned. 'I'm getting married to a woman up country!'

'*Married?*' He felt indignant on Catherine's behalf. 'Does Catherine know about this?' he demanded.

'Oh, yes,' came the casual answer. 'Told her a while ago. She was going to come to the ceremony, but obviously she won't be able to now. You'll have to help her. Take care of her for us.' He slapped Zach on the shoulder. 'I know we can rely on you.'

'Yes. Of course you can,' he replied, stunned by the easy come easy go nature of sexual relationships in Catherine's and Tom's world. 'I think we're done,' he said more briskly. The task ahead was formidable. But he'd rise to it. He felt an odd kind of excitement at the prospect. 'Next job is to prise off the panels I nailed over the windows. Then you can help me to remove the tarpaulin.'

The boat was afloat at last. He and Tom ripped off the panels and manhandled the tarpaulin on to the bank. Feeling as if he were riding on a high, he directed the winch to be set up, securing it to a stout tree. Taking the winch cable and a grappling hook, he paddled in the canoe to the bow of Catherine's boat and fixed the hawser firmly there.

Inch by inch, Steve and Nick sweated to crank the winch and heave the twenty ton boat off the bank where its weight had jammed it deeply into the mud.

Standing on the bank, he waited with bated breath. Beside him, Catherine clasped her hands anxiously.

'It's nearly there!' she squealed, jumping up and down.

Nine hours, he thought proudly. I did it! He punched the air when the boat finally slipped into the horizontal. Dimly he was aware of a ragged cheer from The Boys.

More clearly he felt Catherine's arms around him in a bear hug, heard her gleeful voice, and wished he could live this moment again and again.

'You're wonderful!' she sobbed.

'Hey. No tears,' he muttered huskily, his loins going into melt-down. 'It's hours past lunch-time. How about that curry?'

It was entirely his imagination that she took a long time to detach herself. Then she rubbed her eyes and laughed.

'I go, oh master,' she cried and raced off, to be gathered up by The Boys and thoroughly hugged before they released her.

Zach knew that everything would be an anti-climax from now on. After his insistence that they light Catherine's stove first to begin drying out the boat, they all sat on Tom's barge, wolfing down huge amounts of warm curry and mopping it up with some of Dudley's home-made bread. Steve brought out a bottle of cider and they raised their mugs.

'A toast,' declared Steve. 'To Zach. Well done, mate. It's one hell of an achievement.'

They all shook his hand and clapped him on the back. He smiled, grateful for their friendly praise and suddenly felt perfectly at home with them.

'Thanks for your help,' he said quietly. 'Without you this would have taken all day.'

'Whereas now we've got time to unload before nightfall,' Tom declared, standing up and finishing his coffee. 'Ready everyone?'

Too tired to speak, Catherine surveyed the contents of her boat, which had been ferried by wheelbarrows to the house terrace. The filth horrified her. Her possessions were not only thick with sludge and bits of plant life, but a slick of diesel oil covered everything too.

But there was no time for self-pity. Zach was already wheeling her patient records and papers into the kitchen.

'You wash and I'll dry,' he joked when she came in, her arms full of photo albums.

'Why are you doing this for me?' she asked shakily. 'The boat's up. You didn't have to do more.'

For a moment he looked nonplussed. 'Can't stand the mess out there. Got to get your rubbish sorted out. The sooner we do that, the sooner you're out of my hair,' he replied.

Feeling miserable, she nodded, her eyes widening when he dunked her books into the sink.

'Are you sure you know what you're doing?' she protested in alarm.

'Absolutely. I made enquiries. We can't do proper flood damage renovation. Haven't got the equipment. The next best thing, apparently, is to clean off the muck by immersion, then we interleave the pages with blotting paper and slowly dry them. They'll be a bit crinkly,' he advised, 'because we want to get everything done quickly. Still, you'll be able to read your papers, that's the main thing. Individual papers we can dry directly on the Aga. We'll set up a conveyor belt. It's all a matter of systems and organisation.'

She couldn't help but smile at his efficiency. 'It'll take days to do this lot!'

'We have days. Especially if you use the utility room sink and get on with the photographs.'

'OK.' She moved there and put the plug in the sink, calling out above the noise of the running tap. 'But what about your work—?'

'It's on hold,' he called back. 'I don't do much on weekends, anyway.'

'Oh! I forgot!' she cried, turning off the tap and nervously dunking a wallet of photographs in the water. 'It's getting late. You ought to ring Sam. Kate will be wondering what's happened to you. I'm sure she'd like you to call,' she shouted, trying to feel generous and failing rather badly.

She wanted this incredible man. Wanted to feel his arms about her, to share in his life... He muttered something and she walked to the dividing door.

'What did you say?' she asked.

'I said that I try to avoid speaking to Kate,' he muttered grimly.

She drew in a sharp breath and held it. Her heart thudded loudly in her ears.

'Why?' she asked cautiously.

He seemed very busy with the muddied book suddenly.

'When we divorced,' he replied, 'we agreed that for Sam's sake we'd be civil and friendly. Not avoid one another. Make a point of being affectionate and warm with each other. Kate seems to be taking that a bit far and it bothers me that Sam might think we're getting back together.'

'Aren't you?' she said, her voice near to a squeak.

'Not in a million years.'

Hope rushed through her body, filling her with uncontainable joy.

'I thought...' She swallowed. 'I thought you and Kate were close again?' she breathed.

He scowled into the sink. 'Whatever gave you that idea?'

'She stayed overnight,' she ventured.

He shot her a furious glance, his mouth tight with anger.

'Catherine,' he growled with weary irritation, 'you have to get it out of your head that I haul any passing women into bed!'

'Well...why did she stay?' she persisted, her heart thumping even harder.

'Because we'd talked late. About...various things that were happening in my life,' he retorted. 'She felt too tired to wake Sam and drive back so she camped in the spare room.' He shot her a blazingly angry glance. 'I'd been making love to you,' he snapped. 'Do you honestly think I'm the sort of man to switch my passions so easily and so lightly?' His voice hardened, the line of his mouth growing grimmer with every word that lashed out. 'I'm not fickle. I don't go in for casual affairs. I am not a free spirit, lusting after any woman who crosses my path!'

'No,' she breathed, her eyes sparkling with happiness. 'Of course you're not. I just thought that since Kate had been your wife—'

'I made a mistake where she was concerned,' he said shortly. 'I thought we had a lot in common. Perhaps we did at one time—but now I know we haven't—other than Sam, of course. I no longer want what she wants. We're light years away from each other in compatibility.'

'So...what is it that you want, Zach?' she asked.

His hands stilled in the muddy water. Staring out of the window at the darkened garden, he said quietly, 'I want to live here. To have time and space in my life for my son—and myself, too. To enjoy the small things that make life here so worthwhile and fulfilling. The first rhododendron flower to open. The first sighting of baby ducklings. And to harvest my own vegetables.' He turned to her. 'You opened my eyes to all these things. And for that, I'll be forever grateful,' he said huskily.

She beamed, her eyes misting over. Suddenly the future looked brighter. 'I couldn't be more pleased,' she said simply.

And, standing on tiptoe, she kissed his cheek quickly

before slipping back to the task of swilling silt from each photograph before she pegged them up to dry.

He didn't love Kate, she exulted. But why had he been so distant with her? She yearned for them to be together that night. And possibly for the rest of their lives.

Merrily she unrolled the ball of garden string and fixed lines across the kitchen and breakfast room, carefully hanging up the washed photographs.

Far from being daunted by the task ahead, of cleaning and washing every single paper and all of her belongings, she now felt confident that she could do it. With Zach's help.

Contentedly she worked with him until her head reeled with exhaustion and from the vile smell of glue and size from the sopping papers being dried. She'd had enough. She could do no more.

'That's it for today,' she said, her hand on his arm. 'Come to bed.'

He swallowed. 'Later, Catherine—' he began hoarsely.

Turning his unresisting body around and winding her arms about his neck, she gazed up at him with love in her eyes.

'Now. With me,' she insisted. 'I want to feel your arms around me. To fall asleep with you close by.'

For several seconds he resisted. She could feel the strain as his muscles tensed and began to massage the back of his neck, her eyes never leaving his. There seemed to be some sort of struggle going on in his mind.

'You want me,' she murmured. 'Why hold back?'

He gave a strange kind of laugh. And, although he then kissed her, she felt there had been a bitterness in his eyes just before their mouths locked.

'Why not?' he growled. 'Why ever not?'

Overwhelmed by the sweetness of his mouth and the

depth of her happiness, she took his face in her hands and kissed him passionately.

'We'll need a shower,' she purred.

He began to unbutton her shirt, his breathing short and hard.

'Clothes off here. They're a mess,' he grated.

He captured her mouth, igniting fire within her. Suddenly she wasn't tired any more, only filled with a wild and crazy adoration for him, her senses so inflamed that she astonished herself by stripping off all her clothes and pressing herself wantonly against his half-naked body.

'I want you,' she whispered.

He groaned. His eyes blazed, dark and—for a moment—frighteningly angry. But she must have been mistaken because he bent his head and tenderly kissed her, his hands moving over her body so erotically that she could hardly bear it.

This was different. Almost raw and carnal. But she'd wanted him for so long that his avid hunger matched hers and she felt awed by his need and thrilled that she had aroused it.

His mouth suckled sensually on her neck and she gasped as shudders of pleasure shot through her. His hands slid to her small breasts and cupped them in urgent possession.

She wanted to give herself completely to him. Arching her back, she moaned as his knowing fingers circled her nipples and they grew harder and more erect with every erotic sweep.

'I've wanted this for so long,' he muttered. 'To feel you again. Smell you, taste you. The softness of your skin. The scent of your hair. Your kisses...'

She was weak with longing. Being kissed hard, with a force and a desperation that she'd not known before, she felt herself being lifted on to the table. Her legs twined around his waist and he pressed her back.

Almost immediately she felt the hard, hotness of him against her thighs. His raw fingers teasing her body into moist compliance. The passion of his kisses as they deepened and demanded, his body fevered in its actions—a fever equalled by hers.

'Take me!' she moaned, unable to stand the sweet agony any longer.

'Catherine!' he said in a choked voice.

She kissed him and that kiss was filled with her unbounded love and rapture at being part of him. He slid into her with a groan of release and she shuddered the length of her slender body.

There were no more preliminaries. No teasing, none of the slow driving to a climax. This time he moved fast and hard within her, his mouth and hands fierce and impassioned.

Her fingers twisted in his hair. Her teeth savaged his jaw, his throat, his chest. She caught at his shoulders, her fingers digging into his flesh as she flung her head back and moaned little helpless breathy gasps, her body thrashing about on the hard, ungiving table.

His movements quickened. Slicked with sweat, they surrendered everything—minds, emotions, bodies, to the primitive rhythm. Her brain seemed to be swirling inside and all she knew was that she loved this man and needed to be united with him.

'Catherine!' he groaned, his voice shaking as if he was in agony.

She tightened around him, the sheer pleasure causing her to cry his name, over and over. And surrendered totally to the intense climax that robbed her of breath, of thought, of all consciousness other than the knowledge that she and Zach were as one. And he would always have her heart.

It was a long while before he gained control of himself again. At first he pretended they were real lovers, true lovers. He watched her small face glowing with an inner ecstasy and held her fragile, sensual body in the cradle of his arms. Unable to stop himself, he kissed her. Little butterfly kisses. On her forehead, her enchanting little nose, her mouth and throat. Overcome with emotion he clasped her to him and buried his face in her hair so that she wouldn't see the pain in his eyes.

Because he knew the score where she was concerned. This was sheer pleasure for her. Nothing more.

For his own sake he had to face up to the fact that this relationship might be brief. One day she would fly away like a bird on the wing. Like the swallows who always left the country of their birth.

But for now, she was content to be his. Tom had found someone else and she—so intensely sexual a being— needed a man in her bed and the release of her passions. And he lurched between anger and a helpless understanding that his role had no real meaning for her.

He felt her body relax into sleep. Gently he lifted her and took her to his bed. Her glorious hair writhed across the white pillow as if claiming its place as a permanent right. Her lashes were dark and still and there was a sweet smile on her face.

His stomach contracted. If this was all he could have, then that would have to be enough. Because he couldn't keep away from her. Had to touch her. Kiss the softness of her breast. Inhale the incredible scent of woman.

She'd taken him to paradise that night. His face darkened. And he knew with a chilling certainty that one day she would fling him into hell.

CHAPTER THIRTEEN

'THERE. All done,' she said crisply ten days later, her eyes darting in alarm to the clock above the mantelpiece. So late! She'd over-run again. Her agitation made her frown. 'Come back next week,' she said hastily.

'But...' Her patient sat up, puzzled. 'You didn't work on my arthritis. You always—'

'I'm sorry,' she apologised, already checking through the appointments book. 'There isn't time. Friday at two suit you?'

The woman struggled into her clothes. 'Yes, I suppose so,' she said doubtfully.

'Good. Would you mind letting yourself out?' Catherine asked anxiously. 'I'm in a bit of a rush.'

'Yes, all right, Catherine. Good...bye.'

But Catherine had fled. She had to work all hours now, to earn enough money to do up her boat. As soon as she could, she had to leave.

Zach might want to make love to her every night but he was cold and distant otherwise and very curt with her. She realised where she stood now. He was just using her. They were good in bed together but there was no future for her here.

And so she'd eventually told him she was tired, or had a headache, and had then moved into the spare bedroom.

To salvage her pride and regain her self-respect she must get away from him as soon as possible. He was destroying her, inch by inch.

Zach found the woman in the hall staring blankly at the

passage that led to the back door. He gave a rueful smile. Since Catherine had been using the study as a make-shift consulting room he'd rescued several people from the confusion of corridors.

'You look lost,' he said politely.

'No,' the woman replied. 'I know the way to go. It's just…Catherine.'

He was on the alert at once. 'Something wrong?'

'I don't know. Only that she's different. To be honest,' the woman said, 'one or two of us have noticed that she's less caring since her boat sank. She seems preoccupied. Have you noticed she's always frowning? I suppose it's only to be expected. All that stress. But she's such a sweetie normally. We're giving her the benefit of the doubt, but we're not happy, I can tell you. We pay for a service and expect to get it.'

'You're right,' he said grimly. 'I'll speak to her.'

He saw the woman out, his mouth tight with anger as he strode to the boat, where he'd almost surely find her. Time for a showdown. Catherine had been impossible lately.

He stepped on board and found her jemmying off the last remnants of the once beautifully polished planks which had lined the sides of the boat. With the kitchen units ripped out, together with all the fitted cupboards, the interior of the boat looked bleak and empty. Nothing but an ugly shell.

'A word,' he said succinctly.

'Too busy,' she snapped, heaving a swollen and distorted plank to the floor.

'Not for this. You're being rude to your patients. You can bite my head off if you must, but you have no excuse for venting your spleen on them,' he grated.

Her hand faltered, then she clenched her jaw and continued to apply leverage to the planks.

'I'm perfectly civil to them,' she muttered.

'They're used to more than civility.'

She whirled around, her eyes blazing. 'Well, tough!' she yelled. 'I have no emotional energy left to do any more! I'm working till I drop, here! I've taken on more patients and I do a full day's work six days a week and then I start on the boat! I'm not Superwoman. I can't stay all sweetness and light and keep up that kind of schedule!' she stormed.

'Why do it then?' he hurled back. 'What's the all-fired rush?'

'Because I don't want to stay any longer than I have to!' she flung out.

'I see.' He had the truth now. She was leaving as soon as she could. 'I suppose it's not any of my business if you lose your patients,' he said coldly. 'Live your life as you choose, Catherine—'

'I will!' she yelled, ripping off timbers and hurting her hands in the process. 'Let me get on with my own life, Zach!' she muttered, trying not to cry with the pain. 'You glue that phone to your ear and I'll sort my own boat out—'

'If you'd been aware of me at all,' he said loftily, 'you would have realised that I've cut down my financial activities. I only have a few favoured customers and my own investments keep me solvent. I'm trying to enjoy the beauties of this life—'

'I should be so lucky!' she flung back crossly.

When would she ever have time to herself again? She missed her peaceful moments. There were none of those nowadays. And she felt crabbier and crabbier as the days went on. She turned to make a tart remark to the oh-so-lucky Zach, who didn't have her worries, but he'd gone.

So she flung the jemmy on the floor and stamped her foot like a stupid, frustrated child. Then, because she had no choice, she set to work again, scowling so hard that her head ached.

Dragging herself back to the house, she tried to work out how long it would be before she didn't have to rely on Zach for a roof over her head.

First, the floor had to come up, she'd have to pump out the bilges and rip out the shower and loo then put new fittings back after laying a new floor.

Gloomily she realised that she'd have to take on even more patients from the waiting list. Perhaps do evenings, as well. It was the only way to pay for it all. If she spent the whole of Sundays on the boat, from dawn till midnight, she might just be able to live on board after several weeks.

Too long. There must be another way. Her head lifted. Perhaps there was, she thought. Anything would be preferable to seeing day by day how much Zach hated her.

'She can't still be working!'

'Afraid she is, Sam.'

'But she knows I'm here!' Sam protested. 'She always kept the weekends free—'

'It's different now, son.' He caressed the much loved face of his child, pleased to see that Sam had put on weight. 'Catherine has to earn money to pay for the repairs to her boat. For the wood and new fittings and a new bed and bedding—'

'Is that more important than us?' Sam asked in a small, disappointed voice.

'It's her priority at the moment, yes.' He didn't want

to hurt Sam but he felt angry with Catherine. She knew how much Sam enjoyed being with her. Couldn't she have spared half an hour at lunch-time, instead of racing off to the bank in town? 'Come on,' he said cheerfully. 'We'll make that rope ladder for our tree house.'

They were fixing a climbing net when Catherine finally came along the nearby path. Sam gave a whoop and shinned down to greet her. Zach stayed where he was, his expression cynical.

'Come and see!' exulted Sam, tugging at her arm. 'You've got to try this real cool—'

'I can't,' she said fractiously. 'I've too much to do. Sorry, Sam. Another day.'

She walked on a step or two before Sam stopped staring in dumb amazement and ran up to her again.

'It'll only t-take a moment,' he said, plainly upset.

'Catherine!'

She turned unwillingly and crossly at Zach's commanding tone. 'Yes?' she said, every inch of her body ungracious and defiant.

'Just admire it, will you?' he asked tightly.

Her glance was no more than cursory. It was nothing but a split-second flicker of her eyes. 'Brilliant,' she said shakily. Her mouth trembled as she touched Sam's shoulder in a fleeting gesture. 'Now... Oh, I'm so sorry, sweetheart, but I must go.'

'Dad!'

His teeth jammed together at the plaintive cry and his son's trembling lip. To compensate, he became over-enthusiastic. After a short time, Sam was squealing in delight as Zach 'ahah me heartie'd' himself stupid as they pretended to be rival pirates boarding one another's ships.

Every second he fooled around in an effort to take his son's mind off the cruel snub he felt himself getting angrier and angrier. When Catherine got back he'd give her a piece of his mind. And tell her to get the hell out.

She spent the whole time ripping up her beautiful floor and crying. Not because she had laboured for hours and hours in laying it just six months before the boat had sunk, but because she'd had no time to spare for dear Sam.

She was so on edge she couldn't think straight. Thousands of things to do and to remember. Tiredness washed over her and yet she had to keep going. She had never been more miserable in the whole of her life.

Eventually she could do no more and she made her way back to the house. She disconsolately pushed open the back door and stood in the kitchen hardly able to move another step.

'How dare you?' growled a familiar voice.

Her eyes closed. Not now. She'd scream. She had no patience, no energy for an argument. Her emotions were raw.

'Leave me alone! I'm tired,' she mumbled and began to shuffle to the hall door.

'You'll listen to me!'

She felt herself being dragged bodily along, and then she was pushed unceremoniously into a deep armchair. OK, she thought. She'd fall asleep here—

'Listen to me!'

'Stop shaking me!' she complained hysterically.

Her eyes snapped open. Saw two glowing charcoal eyes filled with hate. Her throat closed up. This was the man she'd once loved. How could she have made such a stupid mistake?

'I want you to pay attention,' he growled, still shaking her.

'I am! I am!' she moaned. 'Just leave me alone! I don't want you to touch me!'

He moved back, his expression contemptuous. 'You don't think I wanted to soil my hands with you, do you?' he snarled. 'I'm doing this because of Sam and for no other reason. I want you to know that you upset him today. You will never, ever be curt or dismissive of him again. Do you understand?'

She put her face in her hands. 'I know what I did,' she whispered. 'And I'm sorry.' She lifted her face. 'Tell Sam I didn't mean to hurt him. I—I care for him very much. Zach, you have to explain.'

'Explain what?' he asked coldly.

'That I am at the end of my tether. I do nothing but work and go to bed,' she said miserably. 'I have never been so tired in the whole of my life. I know I'm short-tempered and snappy but all I can think of is getting enough cash to pay for my boat so I can leave—'

'You've changed, Catherine,' he said harshly. 'Once you were gentle and sweet and thoughtful. You had time and affection for everyone—'

'I could afford the time then!' she wailed. 'I can't now. You must see what it's like for me! You don't think I *like* what I'm having to do, do you? I can see the difference in the way people treat me. My patients are reserved with me now because the atmosphere between us is different. I'm not getting the results I used to and I hate it!' she sobbed. 'But tell me how else I'm to cope? I have to work all hours to make enough or I will remain homeless for the rest of my life. I need time to work on the boat. I'm going mad trying to reconcile the two!'

'I could give you a loan,' he said gruffly.

'No. You're the last person I'd accept help from!' she flared.

'But can't you see,' he snapped, anger flashing from his icy eyes, 'you're alienating the very people you need!

Your patients. Your friends. You're making the same mistake I made. You are working at the expense of your humanity. We've swapped roles, Catherine. And, whatever I think of your morals, I have to admit that you were once a lovely person to know. But not any more.'

'You won't have to worry about it much longer,' she muttered. 'I've been to the bank and I've taken out a loan. I'm leaving tomorrow and taking the boat to a yard for them to do the repairs. I'll dry dock her and get my Boat Safety Certificate at the same time.'

'That's a stupid thing to do!' he raged. 'You could have had the money from me at no interest at all whereas now you'll take years to pay off the debt!'

'It doesn't matter!' she hurled back hysterically. 'At least I'm independent of you!'

Unable to bear his anger and contempt any longer, she ran out and stumbled up to her bedroom, where she mechanically got ready for bed and suddenly fell into a storm of weeping.

She was horrible. A hateful person. Her nerves were in shreds.

Tomorrow, she told herself, she'd be gone. But that thought only made her sob even more. Ahead of her she had the prospect of long hours of work from eight to six or even later in order to fund her frightening debt. And the love of her life loathed her. Little Sam too, probably. She couldn't blame him...

She couldn't bear it. She'd go mad. She loved Zach so much. And no other man could ever match him.

'Catherine, are you OK?' came his stern voice.

'No!' she snuffled into her pillow, in a flash of self-pity.

The bed depressed and she was being rolled over, the air cool on her hot, wet face.

He sighed and then startled her by taking her in his arms. 'I want you to listen to me,' he murmured into her ear.

'Go away!' she moaned.

Ignoring her, he stroked her hair, pushing back the wet strands behind her ears while she sobbed into his shoulder.

'Take *some* time off,' he said gently. 'I know what you're trying to do and I admire you for it. But not the way you're going about it. You're killing yourself. Both physically, mentally and emotionally. You've lost weight and you had hardly any to lose in the first place. You've become a bad-tempered shrew and that's not you. Not the Catherine I l…like to remember,' he said, correcting his peculiar stumble.

'Got to work,' she said crossly.

'An hour here and there won't make much difference. But it will revive your spirits. You know that better than anyone. Why am I having to tell you this? It's all a question of balance, you told me.'

'The difference between us is that you didn't *need* to work so hard. You had enough money. I don't.'

'I know your circumstances are unusual at the moment.' He surprised her by kissing her head. 'But you won't survive long-term if you go on as you are. Let me tell you something. Come on. Snuggle up…'

'Why?' she said sulkily, longing to do just that.

He plumped up the pillows and tucked her into them, slipping off his shoes and curling up beside her. His arm slipped around her shoulders and he drew her into the shelter of his arms. It was blissful. And painful, too. Her hand went out to touch his chest. It would be the last time, she thought mournfully.

'I want to make a difference to your life,' he said huskily. 'Whatever you choose to do, I want you to find that gentle, loving person you once were. You see, my parents were workaholics. And I wish I knew then what I know now. I'm sure they would still be alive.'

'How?' she asked, puzzled.

'Dad was a Thames bargee and took on double shifts. Mum worked in a pub and held down a cleaning job too. I rarely saw them—not because they didn't love me, but because they *did*. They wanted me to have all the advantages they never had. They saved enough to send me to a private school and then I won a place at a top boarding school. Fees still had to be paid, though, and my parents worked even harder. They never enjoyed the small things in life. I'm sure they worked themselves into the ground. When they died I felt I owed it to them to work hard too, and to become successful. Otherwise their sacrifice would have been a waste of time. But I was wrong to think that material success was the only way to judge people, Catherine. It's the kind of person you are that's important. How you treat people. The time you have for others and their problems. You taught me that and I'll never forget what you've done for me and Sam. Don't fall into the trap that I did,' he said softly. 'You're too special for that.'

'I thought you hated me,' she whispered.

'I was angry with you.' He sighed.

'Why?'

'We're from different worlds, Catherine. I don't agree with some of your values.'

'Oh.' Different worlds. There never had been any hope for them.

'Promise me you won't get as scratchy and grouchy as I was,' he said with a rueful smile. 'You'll have frown lines on that beautiful forehead if you go on like this.'

She managed a wavering smile back, but it didn't remain for long.

'OK,' was all she could croak.

'I'll go now. Let you get some sleep.'

'Tell Sam I do care!' she cried suddenly.

'You can do that yourself in the morning. Find time for him, yes?'

'I...I have to leave early,' she choked.

'Then we'll get up to see you off,' he said huskily.

Resolute, he left the room. He felt his heart beating hard but he knew he had to let her go—even though he wanted to beg her to stay. She needed to be free, to claim her independence. To give her body to men she befriended.

She would never be happy tied to a house and one man. Much as he wanted her, he knew that he would rather she left than watch their friendship slowly turn to hatred.

He paused on the dark landing, feeling cold and bleak inside.

'Goodbye, Catherine. Goodbye,' he said in silent farewell.

CHAPTER FOURTEEN

'So, Sam,' she said brightly. 'I'd like to lark around today with you more than anything, and be an enemy pirate, but I have to get my boat fixed. You do understand, don't you?'

His small arms squeezed her waist even more tightly than before.

'Yes, I do,' he said sadly. 'You will come back, won't you?'

'Your father has let me store my things in his shed,' she replied. 'I'll have to call in for them.'

'And then?'

The small face stared at her in a demanding query that was so like his father's that her heart lurched.

'I don't know what I'll do,' she answered in a croak.

'Catherine,' Zach said quietly, 'doesn't plan out her life.'

'Mummy said you were a here today, gone tomorrow kind of person.'

She bit her lip. 'Well I am here today and I'll be gone tomorrow,' she said as evenly as she could. 'So I suppose she's right.'

'Mummy said—'

'Sam!' Zach knelt beside his anxious-looking son, his hand gently rubbing the little boy's back. 'Mummy doesn't know Catherine very well. You must make up your own mind about Catherine.'

'I love her, Dad.'

'I love you, too,' Catherine said, hugging the child. The

moment had come. Somehow she must tear herself away. 'I must go,' she said, choking back the tears. 'Look after Daddy, won't you?'

'You don't want to go,' Sam observed, his lower lip trembling.

'No,' she said honestly, refusing to lie to a child. 'I don't.'

'Is that because you love Daddy and me?' he asked with devastating directness.

She forced an artificial smile. 'Of course!' she cried gaily. 'Zach!' Her eyes pleaded with him to help her escape.

'Right.' He cleared his froggy throat. 'We'll wave madly from the bank. Got everything?'

'Not much to take,' she said ruefully as they marched at a cracking pace towards the boat. 'You're sure you can look after the chickens?'

'Sure.'

'And if you can't handle the vegetable garden—'

'I can. I will.'

'Here we are then,' she announced, appalled at the huge ball of emotion that had stuck in her throat. 'Goodbye, Sam. See you some time.' The little boy hugged her silently and then clung to his father. 'Bye, Zach,' she cried breathily.

He just nodded and waved. So she turned her back on them and cast off. The engine fired and she felt a huge lurch of regret that it didn't immediately splutter to a stop. The exhaust funnel on the roof began to vibrate. There was nothing to prevent her leaving. Staring into the mid-distance, she grasped the tiller and put the boat into gear.

Her wave was directed at Zach and Sam on the bank but she didn't dare to look at them. And as she chugged past the island she felt as if her heart was being rent in two.

Even The Boys' boats were missing. They were still returning from Tom's wedding. She wiped away a tear. She'd write to them. Explain everything.

'Goodbye, island. Sam. Goodbye, my darling Zach,' she whispered.

And gritted her teeth, steeling herself against the void in her heart and the lonely life ahead.

'...Or we could grab a pizza and a video—'

'No, thanks, Dad.'

Zach eyed his disconsolate son helplessly. He didn't blame him. He felt the same. Catherine had gone from their lives and left a gaping hole. They'd tried to amuse one another all day but had failed and were reduced to mooching about the garden pretending to do jobs that weren't really necessary.

'Come and have a cuddle,' he said gently.

Sam flew into his arms. 'I feel miserable,' he mumbled.

'Yeah.' He held his son close. 'I know, son.'

'You love her, don't you, Dad? Mum said you didn't but then, after she got friendly with this man from work and started singing about the house, she suddenly said I was right and that you did love Catherine.'

Zach's thumb tipped up his son's chin. He smiled at the earnest little face and marvelled at the needle-like perception of children.

'Your mother's met someone?' he said. 'I'm pleased for her. It's important for people to find their soulmates.'

'Is Catherine your soulmate?'

He shook his head. 'Unfortunately not. I love her, but she wouldn't be happy with me.'

'Yes she would!' Sam declared hotly. 'She looks at you all dreamy like in films.'

He ruffled Sam's hair affectionately. 'You're willing that to be true,' he said, letting his son down as gently as he could. 'Catherine doesn't like to be tied to anyone or anything.'

'Mum said she loves you,' Sam declared with a child's utter confidence.

Zach smiled. 'Likes me. It's not the same thing.' He looked up at the sound of the doorbell. 'Who's that at this time of night?' he asked.

'Catherine!' squealed Sam, leaping from his grasp.

His heart pounded as he raced after his son, who was dancing up and down in front of the door, demanding it to be opened *now*.

But he knew she wouldn't come to the front door. And so his heart slowed and his hand was perfectly steady when he undid the chain and flung the door open.

'Hi!' said a smiling Tom. Sam burst into tears and hid his face in Zach's side. 'Something I said?' Tom asked, appalled.

'No. Come in. What can I do for you?' Zach pushed the door wide, inviting him in.

'Won't come in. Muddy boots,' Tom said cheerfully. 'Just wanted to invite you over for a drink tomorrow. Seven o'clock. Sort of Coming Home party. And…I wondered where Catherine was. I want her to meet Susie, my wife.'

'Thanks.' He managed a smile for the affable Tom. 'I'd like that. But…Catherine's not here. She's taken her boat to the yard to be fitted out. In any case,' he added with a frown, 'do you think she would have wanted to meet your wife under the circumstances?'

'I don't understand.'

Tom was wide-eyed as if it didn't occur to him that ex-mistresses might find it awkward meeting a new bride.

Zach looked meaningfully at Sam's head. 'You and Catherine were…friends.'

'Still are— Oh! You mean…?' Tom grinned. 'Never! She needs a lot more than mere friendship to…er… develop a more meaningful relationship.'

'That's not how it looked to me,' Zach persisted irritably. Did Tom think he was blind? The least he could do was to acknowledge the truth of what he was saying. 'You and she seemed a lot more than ''friendly'' when I saw you together once. Close. You know what I mean?'

Tom scratched his head. 'Can't think when…' He paused as if something had struck him. Then he laughed. 'Zach, for a clever man, you're a fool! It was after your ex-wife stayed overnight, wasn't it?'

'Yes.' He wasn't so sure he liked Tom's attitude.

'Catherine was upset,' Tom said quietly. 'She imagined…all kinds of things. She cried on my shoulder and I took her inside to calm her down. She was upset, you idiot, because she loves you.'

'Told you, Dad!' piped up Sam's mournful voice.

'I don't think so,' he said tightly.

'Why else would she sob her heart out because she thought you'd betrayed her?' Tom asked. 'She's been crazy about you for ages. We've all seen it, all commented on it.'

'She can't be,' he said hoarsely. 'She hates being tied down—'

'Did she say so?'

He felt his pulses leap. And fought to stay calm and controlled. 'No. But I know that—'

'Listen, Zach,' Tom said, his expression now angry. 'There's no one more moral and upright than Catherine.

In all the years I've known her she hasn't once strayed off the straight and narrow. And I mean in all aspects of life, if you follow my drift,' he added, with a quick glance at the fascinated Sam.

'But…but…'

He couldn't speak. Had he got her so wrong? He wanted to ask questions but his throat was so jammed with emotion that all he could do was gaze beseechingly at Tom.

'She loves you.' The curly head shook in disbelief at Zach's stupidity. 'You're the only one who hasn't realised that. Find Perdita. Go and talk to her. Ask her outright. She won't deny it.'

'Find…*who*?' he asked in amazement.

'Perdita. Her boat.'

He swept a hand over his hair. 'Her *boat!* I don't believe it! I'd totally forgotten…' Perdita, he thought in amazement. Edith, you devious old woman! He fixed his gaze intently on Tom. 'I've got to find Catherine!' he cried urgently. 'I can make her life a lot easier. But I don't know where she is!'

'Then you'll have to search, won't you,' Tom said with a grin. 'Cancel that invitation. You've got some hunting to do. And, knowing your tenacity, I think you'll be successful. Cheers, Sam. See you later.'

'Dad?'

He looked down at his son through mist-filled eyes. 'Telephone book!' he said urgently and they both leapt for it.

If he could do nothing else, he could ensure that Catherine felt financially secure in her own right. The thought of seeing her again both exhilarated and unnerved him, but he had to fulfil the bequest in the will. It would make a difference to her life. Pay off her debts, give her a start towards her future. He would remain perfectly courteous and polite, he and Catherine would exchange pleasantries and then they would go their separate ways.

Carpenters had begun to fit out the interior of her boat in the week since she had left the island. In addition, she had rented a room in a health clinic in Bishop's Stortford at an exorbitant cost and had resumed her practice.

Taking Zach's words to heart, she finished at five in the afternoons and spent her time painting the exterior of the boat to save money. Her debt was spiralling alarmingly and every time she thought of it she went cold inside.

She had begun on the elaborate, traditional lettering on the side of the boat when she heard a voice she knew very well.

The brush slipped. The white letter T smudged and she spent a moment tidying it up and adding the dark green under-shading before she allowed herself to turn.

'Hello, Sam, Zach,' she said, trying to seem cheerful but sounding tight and strained instead.

'I've been looking for you everywhere. And now I've found you and Perdita,' Zach murmured in a self-satisfied tone. 'That's the name of your boat.'

'Yes,' she said in surprise. 'Why?'

'We've got some money for you,' Sam said proudly.

'Very kind. Give it to charity instead,' she replied.

She felt screwed up inside and knew she couldn't keep up her indifference for long. Zach was looking devastatingly handsome in his stone jeans and casual mint-coloured shirt. Her knees felt watery at the very sight of him and her heart was lurching drunkenly inside her ribcage.

'This is from Edith.' Zach held out a package. 'She left

it to you—or rather Perdita—in her will. I meant to ask you a long time ago if you knew who Perdita was. I don't know why I didn't see the name on your boat before—'

'Oh, that's easy,' she replied. 'The bushes on the bank would have hidden it from view. And then I rubbed the panel down ready to be repainted.'

'I see. I'm sorry. It slipped my mind. You could have been comfortably off if I'd remembered.'

She looked at him and the parcel suspiciously. 'You said this is from Edith?'

'Sure. There's a copy of her will inside. You'll see the bequest on page three.'

In silence she opened the envelope and unfolded the will, ignoring the huge stack of notes with it.

'I think,' Zach said quietly, 'she knew you wouldn't accept money for yourself. But this is for the boat. Fifteen thousand pounds. Perdita needs it. You will use it, won't you?'

'Oh, Edith!' she sighed. 'That's a vast amount of money! But how can I refuse her dying wish? Thank you for bringing it to me, Zach. It means I can pay off my debt and set myself up again. I am free of all encumbrances.'

Zach shifted awkwardly. 'Well. That's that, then. We'll be off.'

'No, we won't!' protested Sam.

'Catherine has work to do,' he said sternly.

'But you haven't asked her!'

'Asked me what?' she wondered, replacing the will in the thick envelope.

'Nothing. Sam, you can't embarrass—'

'You do love Daddy, don't you?' he cried plaintively.

'Sam!' Zach scolded as she stared in dismay.

'I want to know!' Sam protested.

Zach put an affectionate hand on his son's shoulder.

'You've put Catherine in a difficult position—'

'Adults are so complicated,' Sam complained.

She found her eyes captured by Zach's. Her pulse began to race. There was so much anguish in his expression that it aroused an answering dart of pain within her.

'Not really, Sam,' she said softly. 'They're just more stupid than children.' She drew in a sharp little breath. 'He's right. I do love you, Zach,' she said shakily and turned back to paint in the A.

'Told you!' said the triumphant Sam.

'Would you mind,' croaked Zach in a hoarse whisper, 'popping off to that shop at the top end of the boatyard and getting me some sweets, Sam?'

'You don't eat sweets, Dad.'

'No. But you do,' he muttered.

She heard the sound of scuffling behind her and then Sam's giggle.

'Oh! Got you!' he said in a stage whisper. 'I'll be a while,' he announced in a loud and utterly false voice. 'Bye for now.'

There was a long silence. So long that she felt the heat of Zach's eyes boring into her back and could hardly see what she was doing.

'What's the matter, Catherine? Are you afraid of commitment?' Zach asked baldly.

'No.' Steadying her hand with the mahl stick, she concentrated hard and moved on to the elaborate scrolls which bordered the boat's name.

'Then why aren't we together, talking about our future?' he asked softly.

She whirled around, paint from the tiny pot in her hand flying all over her. Losing her balance, she fell and crashed down hard on the stone quay.

'Oh, my rear!' she moaned.

'Here. I have some arnica for that,' he said, rummaging in his pocket.

Her eyes opened wide. 'Do you?' Amazed, she took the small bottle and shook out one of the pills.

'Carry them all the time. Did a bit of reading on homoeopathy,' he said. 'I like to have a few emergency items for Sam.'

'That's nice,' she said, her voice wavering as he hauled her up.

'Now,' he murmured. 'Do you worry that life would be too restrictive with me?'

She shook her head dumbly.

'Lost your voice?' he purred.

She nodded.

'Do you think I'd restrict your freedom?'

A shake of the head.

'Would you rather we lived together and didn't marry, so that you felt free to leave any time you want?'

A swallow. Another shake of the head. 'You…you didn't want me,' she finally stumbled. 'Everything was w-wonderful and then you were cold and distant—'

Tenderly he held her trembling shoulders. 'That was due to Kate,' he said. 'That night she stayed. Remember? I told her how I felt about you. That I'd fallen head-over-heels in love with you. She was horrified. And gradually she worked on my doubts, persuading me that you were a free spirit and not the kind of woman to settle down. I felt guilty that I'd made love to you.'

Her eyes opened wide. 'Why, Zach?'

'All the time I wanted to possess you, to have you for myself. And yet it seemed that you didn't want a stable relationship. I realised I'd be caging a wild bird. Kate said I hadn't been fair on you, that I should have seen you only wanted a casual affair. Then I saw you with Tom the next morning when I said goodbye to Kate. You were in his arms—'

'Crying!' she said huskily. 'Over you! Because I loved you and Kate had spent the night with you—'

'I know that now,' he murmured. 'But when I saw you two disappear into Tom's cabin…well that only seemed to confirm everything Kate had said. I thought you treated sex lightly and that I was just one in a long line of your lovers. Which would get even longer as the years went on. I couldn't cope with that, Catherine. So I hardened my heart to you.'

She lifted starry eyes to his. 'I have only had one lover before you,' she breathed. 'It was very serious at the time. You know how it is with young love. But I was seventeen and soon I realised I was in love with the idea of being married and having a family. So we parted, amicably. There's been no one since.'

He took her hands. Knelt on the ground, oblivious of the earth and blobs of paint.

'I will live wherever you want to live. I will be whatever you want me to be. All I ask is that you marry me. I love you more than I can say. I think of you all the time. Dream of you. Conjure up scenes where we are old and grey and greeting our grandchildren. There is nothing in this world I want more than to be your husband. To love you. Cherish you. Make your life perfect. Marry me, Catherine. I know I can make you happy.'

She beamed. 'We could live in the manor. We'll keep it cosy and welcoming and our friends won't be intimidated. The Boys respect you enormously,' she said, her voice shaking with emotion. 'Don't be anything other than yourself.' She smiled. 'And don't stop dreaming of me or imagining our grandchildren. Because I've been doing the same. I love you and admire you and when I'm with you I feel as if I've come home.'

'And...Perdita?' he asked.

Catherine smiled. 'She can be our fun home, for holidays and river trips. For Sam and our children to enjoy.'

'Our children?' he repeated shakily.

'Oh, yes, Zach! I can't think of anything I want more than to be your wife and for you to be the father of my children. I know we'll be happy because every time I am with you I feel pure joy, even if we're doing something ordinary like feeding the hens. The answer's yes, Zach,' she whispered, the tears beginning to form in her huge eyes. '*Yes!*'

He gave a groan, rose to his feet and drew her into a long and impassioned embrace. Somewhere in the distance she thought she heard a cheer. She and Zach looked at one another, startled.

They turned and saw Sam some distance away, jumping up and down in raptures. With him were the yard manager, the shopkeeper and several boat owners she'd befriended.

'Is he going to tell everyone he meets all about our personal business?' Catherine said with a giggle.

'Probably,' Zach answered with a grin. 'Edith met him once. He described the kind of...'

'What?' she asked, wondering why he'd frozen in midsentence.

Chuckling, he shook his head in wry amusement. 'Sam listed all the qualities he wanted in a step-mother. I think that's when Edith hatched her plot. You see, this paragon of a woman he described, fits you to a T. Edith was always on at me to stop working so hard—'

'And she nagged me to find a nice young man!' Catherine laughed.

'The sly old…!' He kissed her tenderly. 'She knew us both well enough to realise we are made for one another. She pushed us together and hoped that time and proximity would do their work. And she even insured against me taking one look at the island and stalking off,' he said ruefully.

'How do you mean?' she murmured, amazed at Edith's deviousness.

'There was a clause in the will which said if I didn't stay for a year then the island and the manor reverted to whoever I first met there. She knew that was likely to be you.'

She gazed at him in adoration. 'She was fond of us both. She knew the island would be in good hands if she left it to you, and that we'd fall in love. Well, that settles it. Can't disappoint her, can we?' she sighed, winding her arms around Zach's neck.

'Absolutely not, my darling,' he murmured huskily and kissed her long and deep.

'Is it nearly lunch-time?' asked a hopeful little voice close by.

They laughed and broke away.

'Yes, Sam!' Catherine said happily. 'Let's go and celebrate.' She drew in a contented breath.

'We're a family now,' Zach said, hugging them both. 'You and your mother and her husband-to-be, you and me and my bride-to-be.'

'Cool!' enthused Sam.

She exchanged a loving smile with Zach. She felt free from her troubles at last. She had everything she could want in the world. Zach and Sam. Perhaps their own children in time. Nothing else mattered.

Just love. Pure and simple.

The world's bestselling romance series.

HARLEQUIN®
Presents~

Seduction and Passion Guaranteed!

Legally wed, great together in bed,
but he's never said…"I love you."

They're…

Wedlocked!

The series
in which
marriages are
made in haste…
and love
comes later…

Don't miss

THE TOKEN WIFE by Sara Craven,
#2369 on sale January 2004

Coming soon

THE CONSTANTIN MARRIAGE by Lindsay Armstrong,
#2384 on sale March 2004

**Pick up a Harlequin Presents® novel and you will
enter a world of spine-tingling passion and
provocative, tantalizing romance!**

Available wherever Harlequin books are sold.

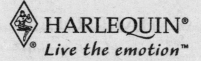

HARLEQUIN®
Live the emotion™

Visit us at www.eHarlequin.com

HPWEDJF

The world's bestselling romance series.

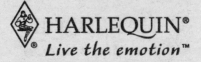

If you enjoyed what you just read,
then we've got an offer you can't resist!

Take 2 bestselling
love stories FREE!
Plus get a FREE surprise gift!

Clip this page and mail it to Harlequin Reader Service®

IN U.S.A.	**IN CANADA**
3010 Walden Ave.	P.O. Box 609
P.O. Box 1867	Fort Erie, Ontario
Buffalo, N.Y. 14240-1867	L2A 5X3

YES! Please send me 2 free Harlequin Presents® novels and my free surprise gift. After receiving them, if I don't wish to receive anymore, I can return the shipping statement marked cancel. If I don't cancel, I will receive 6 brand-new novels every month, before they're available in stores! In the U.S.A., bill me at the bargain price of $3.57 plus 25¢ shipping & handling per book and applicable sales tax, if any*. In Canada, bill me at the bargain price of $4.24 plus 25¢ shipping & handling per book and applicable taxes**. That's the complete price and a savings of at least 10% off the cover prices—what a great deal! I understand that accepting the 2 free books and gift places me under no obligation ever to buy any books. I can always return a shipment and cancel at any time. Even if I never buy another book from Harlequin, the 2 free books and gift are mine to keep forever.

106 HDN DNTZ
306 HDN DNT2

Name	(PLEASE PRINT)	
Address	Apt.#	
City	State/Prov.	Zip/Postal Code

* Terms and prices subject to change without notice. Sales tax applicable in N.Y.
** Canadian residents will be charged applicable provincial taxes and GST.
   All orders subject to approval. Offer limited to one per household and not valid to
   current Harlequin Presents® subscribers.
   ® are registered trademarks of Harlequin Enterprises Limited.

PRES02   ©2001 Harlequin Enterprises Limited

The world's bestselling romance series.

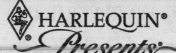

HARLEQUIN®
Presents

Seduction and Passion Guaranteed!

GREEK TYCOONS

They're the men who have
everything—except a bride...

Wealth, power, charm—what else could
a heart-stoppingly handsome tycoon need?
In the GREEK TYCOONS miniseries you have
already been introduced to some gorgeous
Greek multimillionaires who are in need of wives.

THE GREEK TYCOON'S SECRET CHILD
by Cathy Williams
on sale now, #2376

THE GREEK'S VIRGIN BRIDE
by Julia James
on sale March, #2383

THE MISTRESS PURCHASE
by Penny Jordan
on sale April, #2386

**Pick up a Harlequin Presents® novel and you will
enter a world of spine-tingling passion and
provocative, tantalizing romance!**

Available wherever Harlequin books are sold.

HARLEQUIN®
Live the emotion™

Visit us at www.eHarlequin.com

HPGT2004

The world's bestselling romance series.

HARLEQUIN®
Presents

Seduction and Passion Guaranteed!

It used to be just a nine-to-five job...
until she realized she was

Now it's an after-hours affair!

In Love With Her Boss

**Getting to know him in the boardroom...
and the bedroom!**

Available now:
THE BOSS'S SECRET MISTRESS by Alison Fraser #2378
Coming soon:
HIS BOARDROOM MISTRESS by Emma Darcy
March 2004 #2380
HIS VIRGIN SECRETARY by Cathy Williams
April 2004 #2390
MISTRESS BY AGREEMENT by Helen Brooks
June 2004 #2402

Pick up a Harlequin Presents® novel and you will
enter a world of spine-tingling passion and
provocative, tantalizing romance!
Available wherever Harlequin books are sold.

Visit us at www.eHarlequin.com

HPILWHB